ON THE RIVER'S EDGE

Rape, Revenge, and Redemption

A NOVEL

Martha Duke Anderson

For information about special discounts for bulk purchases, please respond to Sales at: mdanderson.5000@gmail.com

On the River's Edge is a work of fiction. Names, characters, locations, and incidents are the products of the author's imagination, are used fictitiously, or are a result of an amalgamation of the author's lifetime knowledge base. Any resemblance to actual events or persons is entirely coincidental.

ISBN 978-0-9988475-2-8 – printed booK
ISBN 978-0-9988475-3-5 – e-book

Printed in the United States of America

Website: www.marthadukeanderson.com

Email:mdanderson.5000@gmail.com

Facebook: https://www.facebook.com/marthadukeanderson/
Author Page

Amazon: www.amazon.com/author/martha.duke.anderson
Author Page

Celebrate: www.facebook.com/groups/1679082692403200/
Golden Images

Twitter: https://mobile.twitter.com/MarthaDA5000

Instagram: www.instagram.com/martha.5000

ACKNOWLEDGMENTS

I gratefully acknowledge the following, whose encouragement and support have been invaluable to me in the writing of this book.

For inspiration, those who whispered this assignment into my mind as I drove west on Highway 84 in July. I would never have thought to do this if left to my own ideas.

For insight into military life and mindset, veterans, fighting, and guns, thanks to my veteran friends: Warren Whitmire, author of *Pale Blue Eyes*; Phillip Moore, owner of Max; and Leeann Brown.

For love, support and encouragement, my dear friends: Scott B. Humble, Dana Lyvers, and Linda Ward– a like mind who knows me so well.

For photographic contributions– Linda Ward, and Max, via Phillip Moore.

And thank you to my group of advance readers.

Special thanks for the cover design by Jeffrey M. Thompson, Jr.

Thank you all!

"We must dare to think about 'unthinkable things' because when things become 'unthinkable,' thinking stops and action becomes mindless."
US Senator J. William Fulbright (1905-1995)

TABLE OF CONTENTS

CHAPTER 1

When a Woman Looks That Good

Look, fellas, it's that Lopez woman," City Councilman Mack Smith said to his morning coffee buddies and softly whistled as they stood outside the River Rock Home Town Diner in the bright sunlight.

"Yummy. Do you think she knows what a turn on she is for us?" Tommy Williams licked his lips as he stared at her. "Look at those curves."

"Now, Tommy," Sam Jones said, "you're the mayor. You're not supposed to talk like that. Some of the ladies who voted for you might not like it. On the other hand, when a woman looks that good, she has to know what she's doing to us men. Look at those three-inch heels. And her little black skirt's at least four inches above those beautiful knees. Why, she's just asking for somebody to do her."

"Well, Sam, you're the prosecutor. You should know, and if she's asking, I'd do her," Mack Smith said. "Wouldn't you, Sheriff?"

"Damn straight I would," Sheriff Jack Raymer said, not missing a beat.

"What about you, young man?" Mack asked Ray Raymer, the sheriff's tall and muscular seventeen-year-old son. He had joined them for breakfast before going to school, to ask his father for some extra money for his Friday night date.

Ray said nothing. All the men were looking at him. He looked at the lady, to his father, and then back to the other men. He nervously laughed a little, smiled, and then loudly blurted out, "Yeah. Shoot yeah, I'd do her!" All the men burst out laughing and patted Ray on the back.

"That's my boy," said the sheriff, grinning.

Angelica Lopez stopped on the sidewalk, turned, and looked directly into the eyes of the sheriff. She didn't bother with the awkward boy who blurted out the comment she heard, nor the other men still laughing from the sidewalk, like common street maintenance workers. She stared into the blue eyes of the sheriff. Her daggers landed, and for a split second, Sheriff Raymer felt what she felt and was embarrassed. Angelica turned away and continued down the street. Mack Smith, watching her hips moving under her skirt as she walked away, stepped up and slapped the sheriff on the back.

"She's got eyes for you, Jack. I believe she wants you." They all laughed.

"Lord knows I want her," the sheriff said. *But there's no way she'll fall in love with me now, thanks to you dim-wit jerks. I'm glad she didn't have a gun in her hand just then. She might have used it.*

Angelica and the sheriff knew each other. Sheriff Raymer had spoken with her many times before. He had thought of asking her out. Since his divorce from Sarah two years ago, he hadn't dated anyone. Angelica had, on many occasions, taken note of the rugged good looks of the tall sheriff, and the tight bulge of his arm muscles beneath his uniform.

River Rock, Alabama nestled up to the banks of the

Muscogee River like a curvy snake hiding amongst the leaves of a flowerbed. It was the county seat of Clayborne County. The old women often told, that the county got its name because the people here were born of clay. Red clay, they said.

The sheriff's office was on Main Street on the city square. Retired from the Marines, Jack Raymer loved the slow, easy-going pace of this small city, his home town. The fast-moving, muddy river and the huge, old, moss-laden trees lining the streets comforted an inner ache. He told his Marine buddies, his city was mostly peaceful, and he mostly just pretended to be a cop.

Jack was in his second term as sheriff of Clayborne county. Sarah Raymer divorced him during his first term, saying she couldn't live with the man the Marines sent home to her.

CHAPTER 2

Hopes and Dreams

Emma Symner and her best friend Hayden Finch sat on the floor in Emma's bedroom. Emma and her white Maltese, Maddy, were playing fetch. "Do you have a date tonight with Ricky?" Emma asked, grinning.

"Yes." Hayden smiled.

"Y'all are together a lot lately, aren't you?"

"We have gotten into an every Friday night date. Sometimes he comes over on Saturday evenings to our house. Momma and Daddy like him a lot. Lately, he talks about things like we'll be together forever," Hayden said. She often walked home with Emma after school and stayed to talk. They found it easier than trying to get Emma's mother to agree to her being late.

"Do you love him?" Emma giggled.

"I think I do," Hayden said, smiling. "He tells me he loves me, all the time." At seventeen, they'd been best friends since the sixth grade when Hayden's family moved to River

Rock. Hayden said they were opposites on the outside but the same inside. She had dark-brown hair and eyes, and tan skin. Emma was blonde, and fair with blue eyes. Each thought the other beautiful.

"Have you done more than kiss?" Emma asked.

"Like what?"

"You know, *it*.... Have you done it?"

"Yuck, no." Hayden blushed. "But sometimes, I let him touch my boobs when we kiss."

"Do you think you'll marry him some day?"

"I think we might marry in the Spring, after graduation," Hayden said.

"Oh my goodness, that's so exciting. I probably won't even date until I'm away at college. You know how Momma is."

"What colleges have you applied to, Emma?"

"The University of Alabama for Daddy, and Auburn University for Momma. You know we are a 'House Divided' on Iron Bowl game day... well, really any day that Auburn or Alabama plays football. I also applied at the University of Alabama, Birmingham campus, for me. I filled out applications for scholarships for them. That's probably what will determine where I go. If I don't get a scholarship, I'll be going to community college and still living here." Emma made a face.

"If you're approved for a full scholarship for all of them, which would you choose?"

"It would break Momma's heart, but I really want to go to the Birmingham campus of the University of Alabama," Emma said, giggling.

"Why Birmingham?"

"They have an incredibly good computer science program there. Then I want to go to Georgia Tech College of computing in Atlanta for a Master of Science degree in computer science. It is one of the best in the world for computer degrees. I want to be a computer engineer and also study software engineering.

"Of course, Daddy would like nothing better than for me to go to work at his office doing income tax returns. Yuck, I would be bored out of my gourd." She crossed her eyes, stuck out her tongue, and pretended to choke herself.

"My folks say your daddy is the best tax man in this area," Hayden said.

"People have told me that, and I'm proud of him. I just don't want to do what he does for the rest of my life. It suits him perfectly though. He's got such a calm, quiet nature about him. He hardly talks at all, but ask him about taxes, and he'll talk all day.

"What about you? Have you decided what you're going to do… besides get married?"

"You know my grades aren't as good as yours, and I haven't done all that volunteering everywhere like you have. My folks insist that I stay home and go to college locally. Things are looking good for me to get a girls' softball scholarship at the community college. They have a great program there. So that's what I'm going to do. But you must get tickets for the Alabama home games and invite me on those weekends. If I'm married and you have a boyfriend, we'll need more tickets!"

"It's a done deal. I've been saving for college with money from my part-time job. Why not spend it all on football game tickets," said Emma, laughing. "That will be so much fun, and we'll be able to still be close. Maybe I could come home sometime when you have a game. I'll come cheer for you! There ought to be some old pom-poms around here somewhere." They laughed.

"I almost forgot! I gotta go home and get ready for Ricky. I'll call you tomorrow."

CHAPTER 3

From Way Back

Hey, Jack," Alabama State Senator William Bradford said as he nearly ran into Sheriff Raymer who was walking out the side door of the stately, old Clayborne County Courthouse. A home town man, most of the locals called him Senator Billy.

"How are you, Billy?" Jack asked.

"I'm doing well. Say, Jack, I've been meaning to pay you a visit. I want to talk with you about something."

"What's on your mind? You want to sit here and talk?" He motioned to one of the benches across the street in the square.

The courthouse, sheriff's office, and other businesses sat on the outside of the town square. A lush, green park filled the inside. Huge, old, oak trees shaded the walk-ways and benches. Moss hung from most. A sprinkling of red bud trees, crape myrtles, dogwoods, and azaleas added seasonal color to the park. Huge baskets of blooms hung from each of the black-iron light posts throughout the park. A beautiful fountain was the square's focal point. On the center pedestal, stood a graceful maiden looking to the heavens with outstretched arms.

"Let's do. I have a little extra time before Sherry expects me for our Friday date night," the senator said.

"Y'all still do that? I'm impressed."

"Sherry insisted on it a long time ago. I'm away so much. That's the tradeoff. We can't always do it, but if I'm home, it's a standing date."

"I think it's great," said Jack, as they found seats. "So, what's up?"

"Jack, with me being out of town so much, I know we haven't gotten together very much since you retired from the Marines, but we go way back. We've known one another since we were little kids. Maybe you'll let me pick your brain a bit. I haven't told many people, but I'm thinking I might run for governor one day. I'd appreciate it if you don't talk with anyone about it until I announce I'm running, and I really don't know when that will be. I'm just playing with the idea in my mind.

"I was thinking about a campaign platform. I'd like to be the candidate known for being tough on crime. That's where you come in, Jack. I'm hoping you might help me with some ideas I could use in my campaign. After you have some time to think about it, maybe we could get together and talk more. What do you think?"

"It sounds to me like you're running, Billy. I think you'll make a fine governor, and I'll be glad to help you any way I can. Who knows, if you're the governor, you might help our city with some projects," Jack said as he noticed Angelica Lopez walking down the sidewalk toward them. She hadn't yet seen them tucked back off the sidewalk in the shade of an ancient oak. Billy saw Jack watching her.

"Do you know her, Jack?"

Jack threw his hand up in a wave, "Good afternoon, Angelica," he called to her. She looked at him and then straight ahead, saying nothing. His smile faded.

"Hey, she's Hispanic, isn't she, Jack? Maybe you and she could go out to dinner with me and Sherry sometime. Just having her in a photo with me might help me with the Hispanic voters! Let's do that sometime!" Senator Billy said.

Jack's eyes trailed after her, while Billy rattled on about voting demographics. Jack had enjoyed Angelica's sweet smiles as she walked by each morning. He saw goodness in her eyes and wondered if he could ever again be worthy of the love of someone like her. He didn't think so, but he liked fantasizing about being close to her and holding her. When she was still speaking to him, it had seemed possible. As Angelica rounded the corner, leaving his sight, he felt his heart longing to be near her and fought the urge to follow her.

"I got so wrapped up in our conversation, I almost forgot my date with Sherry. I better hurry home, but I'll be back by to see you soon, Jack. Thank you for talking with me. I can hardly wait to hear your ideas."

"You and Sherry have a good evening, Billy."

CHAPTER 4
Wrong Place, Wrong Time

I t is so dark out here," Emma muttered to herself. "Why don't they put up some lights on this road?" She was driving outside the city on Riverside Road along the Muscogee River. Dark clouds tumbled across the sky, hiding the light of the moon. Tall trees lined both sides of the dark pavement. She slowed the car a little.

I'm going to kill Noah when I find him, Emma thought. She had been the peacemaker between her brother and mother for years. Noah, at sixteen, was only a year younger, but he didn't always act his age. Emma had volunteered to look for him when Gayle, their mother, pitched a fit because it was long past the time Noah was supposed to be home. Emma thought Noah and his friends might be out here at the place the teen-agers called, 'the playground.'

Slowing the car now to a crawl, Emma looked for the turn-off to the overgrown dirt trail going into the woods. She turned onto the trail which led to a clearing on the banks of the river. No one seemed to know the owner of the property, and none of them were about to ask their parents. A picnic table and lawn chairs had accumulated there over time. Late-night fires often burned when the teenagers were there. They brought their music and ice chests with drinks. Some of the kids occasionally brought beer and blankets.

Emma was relieved to see the light of the fire up ahead. "Great, they're here," she whispered to herself. She pulled slowly into the clearing and turned off her car. A large muddy truck with big tires pulled in and stopped on the trail road behind her car. "Now, who is that blocking me in?" She jumped out of her car, heading toward the fire, and suddenly stopped, noticing these people were strangers. They were rough-looking grown men.

Everything went black. Emma screamed, thrashing her arms about. Someone behind her had put a black t-shirt over her head. It reeked of body odor, beer, cigarettes, and a faint bit of Old Spice. Someone grabbed her arms from behind. The shirt was pulled tightly around her eyes and tied behind her head.

"Get those zip-ties, Bert," someone said. Bert tied her wrists behind her.

"Let me go! What are you doing? What do you want?" she yelled, struggling.

"We want you," a deep, calm voice said. Panic washed over her. She screamed again, calling for help. The area was isolated. No one heard her cries except the men surrounding her. She heard only the gentle lapping of the river until one of the men started laughing.

"Oh my God in heaven, help me," she prayed aloud. She continued yelling for help. "Please don't," she begged. "I'm a virgin," she said, crying.

"Dougie, shut her up," Carl Mitchell ordered.

"Right, Carl, okay. What do you want me to do?"

"Use that duct tape on the table over there. Bert, Vince, hold her down. Ned, help them."

Terrified, Emma kicked and struggled. Someone punched her hard in the face and then kicked her in the stomach. The duct tape stopped her calls for help.

"Paul, Oliver, get her feet. Y'all bring her over here to the table," Carl ordered.

Oh my God! Jesus, please help me, Emma thought, over and over again.

"So, we got us a virgin here. Excellent work, boys," Carl said. "Give me that knife. Let's get these clothes off and see what our sweet little virgin looks like." He sliced her clothes with expert precision. Emma felt him next to her leg and kicked him as hard as she could. Like a reflex, he reached up and slapped her hard across the face, letting his hand slowly slide back down her naked body and pinching her nipple. He laughed, the same laugh she'd heard earlier. "It looks to me like we don't have a sweet little virgin here after all. Nope, I think she's a rich, bitch, blonde, cheerleader who thinks she's too good to spend time with the likes of us. And it won't be long before she'll be a bitch of a momma who's never satisfied with anything. Don't you think so, boys? Maybe we should show her just how much fun she can have with us. Any of y'all ever wanted to fuck the stuck-up head cheerleader who always called you names? Well, now's your chance, fellas. Time to show this stuck-up cunt we're the boss, and now, we take what we want!" Emma whimpered, trying to beg through the tape.

Carl was first. "There goes that rich bitch cherry," he yelled and beat his chest. The others cheered. His thrusts were hard. "Here, take this, bitch momma. See if this is good enough for you." The tape muffled her screams. He stopped, took his leather belt, turned her over the end of the table and whipped her butt and back, drawing blood, telling her how bad she had been and that she needed to be taught a lesson. Emma cried in pain. Then he sodomized her. Her scream was barely audible through the tape. All the others raped and sodomized her, each calling her a bitch and other names while Carl egged them on. They all clapped, whistled, and cheered each man's performance. Emma kicked at them, and with each kick, she was beaten a little more. She had weakened, but made one last feeble kick. It was followed by a particularly hard blow to her head, and left her unconscious. They kept at it anyway. She was limp like a rag doll. They rode out, leaving her there, naked, bloody, still tied up, with the shirt over her face, not moving.

❖❖❖

Noah had gotten home about an hour after Emma left looking for him. He and his mother had argued. He wasn't allowed to go looking for Emma, but she didn't come home. After three hours, Gayle had called the police. They couldn't file an official missing person's report so soon but came to the Symner residence and collected information and a photograph of Emma. They passed copies of it along to all their patrolmen and to the county sheriff's department, asking everyone to be on the lookout for Emma and the car she was driving. Gabe spent the rest of the night driving around, looking for his daughter.

❖❖❖

"Where am I?"

"You're in the hospital, honey," said a middle-aged nurse with bags under her eyes. "What's your name, sweetie?"

"Emma Symner. How did I get here?" Tears began to stream from her eyes.

"I was told, someone found you and called 911. They brought you in on an ambulance."

The nurse hurried away to notify her supervisor of Emma's name. She returned and a rape kit was used to collect semen samples for DNA testing and other forensic evidence. Photographs were taken of the injuries all over her body. Emma shook. The hospital was cold.

"I'll get you a blanket," the nurse said and brought back two.

"I need that pill to keep me from getting pregnant," Emma told the nurse. "That morning-after pill, I think it's called."

"Sweetie, the laws were changed, and that pill is no longer available for us to give you," the nurse said.

"But I was raped," Emma said. "Please, it wasn't my fault. I fought them."

"I'm sorry, honey. We don't have it here anymore to give to you. I'm sorry. It's against the law to use that pill now."

"I was a virgin. Please, I don't want to get pregnant. I'm going to college after I graduate high school. Please don't let me get pregnant by those scum bags," she begged. "You can see, I fought them. I was raped... I was raped." Emma sobbed.

❖❖❖

A policeman arrived at the Symner home. Gabe and Gayle saw the policeman at the door and thought Emma was deceased. He explained, a girl with no identification, but matching Emma's description, was in the hospital. The car at the scene was registered to Gabe Symner.

❖❖❖

Gabe, Gayle, and Noah Symner waited outside the emergency room. They'd had no sleep the night before. A sheriff's deputy and a doctor met with them.

"An old man out on Riverside Road found your daughter and called it in," the deputy said.

"I'm sorry," the doctor said. "Your daughter's been raped and badly beaten. When you're ready, I'll take you to her. We've done x-rays and tests. There's nothing that will require her to stay here. We'll watch her a few more hours, and you can take her home."

Please note: This book of fiction includes an imagined future time in which the morning-after pill has been made illegal. This is not factual information as of this book's published date.

CHAPTER 5

The Victim Interview

Hello, Miss Symner, Mr. and Mrs. Symner, young man. I'm Sheriff Jack Raymer. I'm sorry we're meeting under these circumstances," the sheriff said as he entered the hospital room, which smelled of disinfectant.

"This is our son Noah," Gabe said and shook hands with Sheriff Raymer. Noah, who sat cross-legged on the floor, glanced up and then back to the spot on the baseboard, which he thought looked like a grizzly bear devouring a fish.

"I need to hear from your daughter what happened last night," the sheriff said.

"Well, she went looking for Noah last night, and she got raped," said Gabe. The blood drained from his face. He reached out for the chair next to him and eased himself into it.

"Yes, sir. I understand that, but I'm going to need to hear everything from Emma. One of you can stay while I talk with her, if you want."

"I'll stay," Gayle said.

"I'll take Noah to lunch and bring something back for you," Gabe said as he picked up his newspaper and jacket and left the room.

❖❖❖

Sheriff Raymer pulled a chair to the side of the bed. Emma told the sheriff what happened the previous night. The sheriff jotted down notes in a small notepad from his breast pocket.

"Miss Emma, what was a young girl like you doing out in the woods after dark?"

"Like my husband told you, she was out looking for her brother who was late getting home," Gayle answered.

"I see. What clothes were you wearing last night, Miss Emma?"

"I had on blue sweatpants and a long-sleeve blue t-shirt," she said. "But I don't see what that has to do with what happened to me."

"I'm just collecting information," said the sheriff. "Miss Emma, do you have a boyfriend?"

"I have a good friend who is a boy but we're not really dating, and he didn't have anything to do with this," Emma snapped back.

"You said you were unable to see any of the men, is that right?"

"Yes, that's right."

"Then how do you know he wasn't there?"

"When I first got out of my car, I didn't see their faces, but they were all big, grown men. My friend is slender like a teenager and not like a man. I could hear them talking, and he wasn't there."

"What is your friend's name and address, Miss Emma?"

"I told you it wasn't him," Emma said. "His name is Bob Theron." She gave the sheriff his address.

"Then it will be easy to eliminate him as a suspect," said the sheriff. "Have you and your boyfriend had a fight recently?"

"No, we haven't! And I told you, he isn't my boyfriend."

"Miss Emma, why would you go to such an isolated place, by yourself, after dark? Were you planning to meet someone there?"

"No! I told you already, I was looking for Noah and thought he might be there."

"Really, Sheriff Raymer, we have told you this before, and she doesn't have a boyfriend," said Gayle.

"So, you didn't see any of their faces?" Sheriff Raymer asked.

"No, I didn't."

"Did you go to your last prom, Miss Emma?"

"Yes, I did."

"Who took you to prom?"

"Bob Theron," Emma said, looking at her mother and shaking her head.

"I see," the sheriff smiled. "Miss Emma, when you went out in the woods, alone last night in the dark, got out of your car, and walked toward the men, how did you act?"

"Are you out of your mind?" Emma yelled. "Do you really think I went there and was coming on to those men? You think I caused this? Look at my face! Do you think I asked for this? They raped me, Sheriff!"

"I go to church every time the doors are open. I sing in the choir. Aside from prom, I have never been on a date without other people with me. I was a virgin until last night. I was saving myself for marriage.

"How did I act? Someone put a black t-shirt over my head from behind, and I screamed. I tried to get away. They zip-tied my wrists behind me. See these cuts and bruises on my wrists. They beat me with a belt that cut into me. They took turns raping and sodomizing me! How did I act? I kicked at them and every time I did, they beat the hell out of me until they knocked me unconscious! That's how I acted. The nurse took pictures of all these cuts and bruises. Didn't you see them? You think all this is my fault? How could you?" Emma and her mother were both crying.

"Well, Miss Emma, if we find anything, we'll be in touch. Frankly, it will be difficult to prosecute anyone because you cannot identify any of the men. If you think of anything else, just let us know." The sheriff put his notepad and pen back in his shirt pocket and walked out.

"Momma, when they brought me to the hospital, the nurse used one of those rape kits to collect evidence like DNA. She was nice and explained everything to me. She even cut my fingernails and put them in a package in case there might be DNA under my nails. Maybe that will identify the men."

"Maybe so, sweetheart. I hope so," Gayle said, blowing her nose.

"Momma, they wouldn't give me that morning-after pill to prevent pregnancy," Emma was still crying. "Momma, what if I get pregnant?" she sobbed.

Her mother sat on the bed, put her arm around Emma as gently as she could, trying not to touch her injured places, and told her, "Don't worry about that. Everything's going to be all right. I'm thankful the good Lord has brought you through this and back to us." Gayle dabbed Emma's tears with a tissue.

CHAPTER 6

Senator Billy Will Help

Singing *Amazing Grace* at the Greatest Love Baptist Church, Gabe tapped Gayle on the leg and pointed to Senator Billy taking a seat on the cushioned pew across the aisle. The senator was attending church with his wife and children. During the week, he worked at his office in Montgomery, Alabama, home of the ornate state capital building.

"Let's talk with him about Sheriff Raymer," Gabe whispered to Gayle. They had left Emma and Noah at home. Emma was still black and blue, and very sore. Gayle had instructed Noah to take good care of her and get her anything she needed.

Pastor Robert Stevenson stood at the large wooden pulpit positioned in the center of the raised platform. "Please remember, in your prayers this week, our members going through illness, our elderly shut-ins, and a special remembrance in your prayers for one of our young members who has been violently assaulted. We know and affirm that the good Lord never puts more on us than we can bear. Please bow your heads now for our morning prayer."

After the closing prayer, Gabe asked Senator Billy for a private talk. Gabe, Gayle, and the senator met under one of the shady old oak trees on the side of the church.

"Billy, that was our daughter Pastor Stevenson was talking about earlier. Some men beat and raped our little girl." Gabe's voice broke, and he turned away. After fishing in his pocket for his folded white handkerchief, he wiped his eyes, blew his nose, and turned back toward the senator.

"I'm sorry to hear that, Gabe. Is there anything I can do to help?" Senator Billy asked as he laid his hand on Gabe's shoulder.

"The sheriff was awful when he questioned Emma," Gayle said. "He acted like the whole thing was her fault and asked her stupid questions like 'What were you wearing?' and 'Do you have a boyfriend?' Then he as much as told her there's nothing he can do because she didn't see the faces of the men, even though the hospital gathered DNA. He has just dismissed the whole thing. He doesn't want to catch them."

"Would you like me to talk to him about it?" Senator Billy asked.

"Yes, Billy. Anything you can do to help get justice for our daughter will be much appreciated," Gabe said. "She's afraid to leave the house; she's afraid of running into them again."

❖❖❖

Emma, still in bed, had no desire to get up. She felt tired. She still hurt every time she moved. She flipped her pillow over to the cool side and nestled her face into its softness. She smelled the faint residue of bleach, a scent which meant it was clean. Here she was warm, comfortable if she didn't move, and most of all, she felt safe.

"Emma, want to play cards?" Noah asked from her door.

"No."

"Want to watch a movie?" He was now at her bedside.

"No."

"Want me to get you some cereal or fruit?"

"No, leave me alone. Get out!" Noah lowered his head, staring at the floor.

"Emma, I'm sorry I wasn't home and that happened to you. It wouldn't have happened if I had been home on time." Noah fell to his knees beside Emma's bed, "I'm so sorry. It was all my fault." Tears slid down Noah's face.

Emma reached out with both hands and cupped his cheeks. "Noah, it wasn't your fault. You are not responsible for what happened. I'm sorry I yelled at you. I'm just not myself. I'm tired, and I hurt all over."

"Want me to get you one of the pain pills the doctor pre-scribed for you?"

"Not right now. Maybe a little later. Did Momma and Daddy go to church?"

"Yes, but I'll get you anything you want. Just ask. Momma said they will pick up a bucket of chicken on the way home. She made a peach cobbler before she left, and there's ice cream in the freezer. She told me not to touch it, but she won't mind if you want some now."

"Thanks, Noah. I'll wait until they get home and eat with y'all. Let me rest until then."

"All right. Call me if you want anything." Noah turned the light off again and closed the door.

Emma lay in bed thinking. Then she slowly rolled over and eased herself from her bed to the carpeted floor. Elbows on her bed, she pressed her hands together in front of her face. Light shone into the darkened room from the window.

"Heavenly Father, I love you. I've always been a good girl. I've been kind, and always tried to do what's right and what I thought you'd have me do. Why did you let this happen to me? I don't understand why this happened. Please help me understand and make peace with this. I don't want to hate anybody, but… I hate those men who did this to me. Please forgive me and help me forgive them. Help me, Father, please. I feel so lost, and I feel such hatred for those men, and even for the sheriff for the way he treated me. I pray the sheriff learns to better understand all of this, and he treats others in my situation better. I pray there never be another rape of anyone. And please, please, don't let me be pregnant. In thy name, Amen."

Emma pulled a tissue from the box on the bedside table, wiped her tears and climbed back into bed. She took her favorite position on her left side, slightly curled, and her mind retreated into its sanctuary.

CHAPTER 7

Politics Gone Awry

Good morning, Jack," Senator Billy said. It was Monday morning, and the senator was stopping by the sheriff's office before leaving for his Montgomery office.

"Good morning, Billy. What brings you by again so soon?"

"I was talking with Gabe and Gayle Symner yesterday. They're upset about their daughter's incident. I wanted to hear how the investigation's going. They seem to think nothing is being done toward finding the rapists of their daughter. They think you've been insensitive and uncaring about the whole thing."

"Well, Billy, the girl didn't see their faces. She can't identify any of them. She can't pick them out of mug shots or work with a sketch artist. What do you want me to do, call a damn psychic? Maybe somebody could read the leaves in her tea cup."

"What about the DNA test, Jack? They said she went to the hospital."

"She did. But there's a long backlog for rape kits. Those things don't get processed in a timely manner. This is your area, Billy. The state crime lab's budget has been cut, and some of the labs have been closed. Those test kits have been piling up for years, from lack of funding. There are thousands of them unprocessed in our state, and it's the same all over the country. The bad thing is a lot of perps are serial rapists. If we could get them off the street, it would keep others from being raped. Mobile and Birmingham got grants to help process their backlogs. They're big cities. We're not."

"I had no idea this was happening," said Senator Billy.

"After Mobile got its grant and started testing, they prosecuted a man who raped a woman twenty-four years ago. She's eighty-one now and testified in court. The rapist was a stranger who kicked in her back door in the middle of the night."

"Well, this is something I didn't know about, Jack. I can certainly see where you're coming from. So, let's think this through a bit. If the Symners keep telling people you're not doing your job, that won't look too good to the public. I'm thinking it might help us both if we go out there to the crime scene together, come back here, and then do a press conference about trying to solve this crime. We could also ask for tips from the public. That might help us both come time for re-election. What do you think?"

"I guess it wouldn't hurt to go ahead and get started with the ole dog and pony show. All right, I'm in. I'll have my assistant call the area TV stations and newspapers while we're gone and tell them what time to be here. We can figure out what we're going to say on the way there and back. Remember, Billy, the victim's name isn't to be released. Don't tell her age either. You know the kids will know who has missed school and then returned with bruises. I'm free now. Let's take my patrol car."

"It's about five miles outside the city," said the sheriff as he drove. "It's an isolated spot off the road by the river. It's a wonder something hasn't already happened out there. The kids have evidently been gathering there to party for quite a while."

"That's why she was there?" asked Senator Billy.

"No, she was looking for her little brother and found trouble instead, with some grown men."

"So, she didn't stand a chance," said the senator.

The sheriff turned off the road onto the dirt trail going into the woods. The trees surrounding the road formed what any other time might have seemed like a beautiful canopy of foliage. Today, it seemed a dark and foreboding place.

They rounded a curve and saw a black F-250 Super Duty Lariat FX4 off-road truck parked in a little clearing to the right. Its bottom half was coated in mud, and the rest was well spattered. It was high off the ground and sported big Mud Gripper tires.

A little farther around the curve, motorcycles were parked to the left of the trail. Ahead, a clearing opened up just before the banks of the Muscogee River. As the patrol car pulled in, several men who had been sitting on a picnic table stood and took a few steps toward the car. Carl Mitchell, in a black leather vest, rose from a lawn chair. The sheriff and the senator got out of the patrol car and walked toward the men.

"What are you all doing here?" asked the sheriff.

Carl Mitchell stepped forward. "We're a motorcycle club," he said. "We've been out riding and just stopped to rest a while."

"What's the name of your motorcycle club?" asked the sheriff.

Carl Mitchell couldn't think of a name. "We don't have an official name," he finally said. "We're just friends who like to ride."

"Then what's your name?" asked the sheriff.

"I'm Carl."

"Carl who?"

"Carl Mitchell," he said, getting irritated.

"Do you own this land, Carl?"

"No, I don't," Carl said.

"Then you all are trespassing here, aren't you? Let me see your identification," the sheriff ordered. The senator stood about three feet behind the sheriff near the patrol car, rocking back and forth.

"Look, Sheriff, we're just chilling out here. We're not hurting anybody. We can leave if you want."

"What I want is to see all of your IDs," the sheriff said. "And where were you a week from last Friday?"

"We would have been out riding somewhere," Carl said with a smirk.

"I'm going to need you all to come downtown to the sheriff's office and answer a few questions."

"We've made some other plans for this afternoon," said Carl. "Maybe some other time."

Senator Billy stepped forward. "You see, gentlemen, a young girl was assaulted out here, and we're just trying to get to the bottom of it. Maybe you can help."

"Hey, dude in the suit, you're that damn politician that was on TV promising everybody would have jobs if you were elected, ain't you?" Ned yelled.

"I have been on television a few times," Senator Billy said.

"Let me see your identification," the sheriff said, looking at Carl Mitchell.

"No, I don't think so," Carl said.

"Look, boy, hand me your driver's license if you know what's good for you."

"I ain't your damn boy, you bastard. And if you know what's good for you, you'll climb back into your car and drive away from here right now."

Sheriff Raymer took a couple of steps forward. Carl Mitchell did the same. Senator Billy took a step backwards. Carl Mitchell's band of brutes instinctively eased in closer, surrounding all three.

"Who do you think you are, talking to the sheriff of Clayborne County like that?" Sheriff Raymer asked.

"Jack... Jack... come on. Let's just go. Let's go!" Senator Billy said.

"You better listen to your pansy-ass senator friend and

go. You're the one who came up in here asking for trouble. I can give you trouble all right," Carl said.

"I told you to show me your damn driver's license, boy, and I'm going to see it one way or another," Sheriff Raymer said.

Carl Mitchell lunged forward toward the sheriff and swung with his right hand. The retired Marine turned sheriff ducked the swing, and counter-punched, hitting Carl in the mouth with a cross punch. His blow was so hard, it busted Carl's lip and knocked out a tooth. The sheriff grabbed Carl's wrist and hand, spun him around and downed Carl face-first into the dirt.

The senator had been steadily stepping backwards on the way to the driver's side door until Ned and Oliver came up behind him, each together kicking him on the back side of his knees, making him fall forward into the mud in his freshly cleaned suit pants.

The sheriff had allowed his body to fall forward knees first into the back of Carl Mitchell. "Not so damn cocky now, huh?" the sheriff said. He reached behind him for his hand-cuffs just as Vince hit him over the head with an empty Jack Daniel's bottle. The sheriff fell to the ground, dazed.

Paul helped Carl to his feet. "Get the son of a bitch up! Get him up!" Carl snarled.

"You don't have to do this. You don't have to do what-ever you're thinking. You can stop it all now and go," Senator Billy said.

"Shut him up," Carl ordered. Bert brought over duct tape and applied it to the senator's mouth. Paul zip-tied the wrists of the sheriff and the senator. Their hands were behind their backs. Dougie and Paul moved the still-dazed sheriff to a lawn chair. Bert brought the tape for the sheriff's mouth.

"Bert, no," Carl said. "Wait on that. Bring me that small

ice chest," he said as he wiped at his bleeding lip. The sheriff's eyes were closed. His head nodded side to side.

Carl opened the ice chest, and took out the last few beers. He opened one, took a swig, swished it around with the blood in his mouth and spit it on the sheriff. He poured the remaining ice and water over the head of the sheriff. "Wake up, smart ass," Carl said and slapped him open-handed. The sheriff's eyes fluttered and opened. He saw the senator on his knees, tape over his mouth, with Ned and Oliver positioned on either side.

"You best cut these ties, boy. You're getting in way over your head here."

"I done told you, I ain't your boy, you son of a bitch." Carl slapped the sheriff again, harder this time.

"The rest of you boys, y'all are going to be accessories to anything Carl here decides to do. You know that, don't you? You all want to go to prison?" Carl slapped him again.

"You think you're such a big, tough man. You're not so tough now, are you?" Carl yelled and slapped him again.

"Carl, man, come on, let's just go. I don't want to go to prison, man," said Paul. Carl glared at him, "Paul, you're a damn wuss."

"Your troops are turning on you, Carl. You're no better at leading them than you are anything else," said the sheriff. "You must be the one who attacked that young girl out here. What's wrong, you can't get it up for a girlfriend your own age?" the sheriff taunted.

"I can get it up for anybody, anytime! I can show you, and you've never seen a bigger dick than mine. Paul, Bert, get over here. Get him over to the table. Dougie, Vince, help them."

"Carl, come on, man, don't do that. Let's just go," said Paul.

Carl whirled around, eyes wild, "You and all the rest of you are gonna do what I tell you, or I'll kill you. You got that? Now get him over there. He thinks he's such a big, tough man. He thinks we're nothing. We'll show him who's in charge here, and it ain't him. Ned, Oliver, bring the damn senator closer so he has a better view."

They did as they were told. The sheriff was backed up against the picnic table. Carl Mitchell gut-punched the sheriff, hit him in the right eye, the left, and then the stomach again. He stepped back. "Take his belt off," he said.

Carl put the sheriff's belt around his neck and pulled it tightly from behind. "Take off his pants," he ordered. As Vince and Dougie pulled them down, Carl jerked the belt, pulling the sheriff backwards onto the table and his legs up into the air. Paul and Bert helped. His shoes, pants, and boxers were removed, with the sheriff cursing and kicking. They took off his shirt.

"Get your damn hands off me," the sheriff yelled.

"You're not in charge here, I am," Carl yelled back. "You like talking down to people. You think you're so tough. You think we're nothing but low-life trash. You're not so tough now, are you? Who's in charge now? Say, 'You are, Carl.' Go on, say, 'You are, Carl.'"

"Fuck you! You son of a bitch!" the sheriff yelled.

"No, we're going to fuck *you*, you pussy-ass sheriff! We're all going to fuck you."

"You lay one hand on me for that, and I swear to God, I'll kill every damn one of you. Do you all hear me? I'll kill you every one!"

"Sheriff, hush now. Remember, I need to prove I can get it up anytime I want. Oh, and that it's the biggest you've ever seen. It'll be the biggest you've ever felt too."

"Don't do it. I'll kill you if you do!"

"Tough guy, Sheriff. I'm about to tear your ass up," Carl said laughing. "After all, you knocked my tooth out. I think I deserved a big fuck in return, don't you?"

"You want some of this duct tape for him, Carl?"

"Not just yet, Vince. I want to hear him a while longer," said Carl.

"I'm going to kill you all," said the sheriff.

"Turn 'em around and hold 'em down," Carl said. He took off his own leather belt and beat the sheriff with it, on his back and butt, just as he had Emma. Carl yelled taunts at him.

The sheriff didn't make a sound throughout the beating. In his mind, he repeated a mantra over and over again, "Carl-Paul-Bert, Dougie-Vince-Ned, and Oliver. Carl-Paul-Bert, Dougie-Vince-Ned, and Oliver." His eyes were closed. He was in some far-removed place.

Carl moved behind him and penetrated the sheriff as hard and as suddenly as he could. Jolted back, involuntary sounds escaped from the sheriff. Carl pulled on the end of the sheriff's belt, looped around his neck. He choked the sheriff as he rammed into him again and again and again. The sheriff's big bicep muscles flexed, and blood ran down his hands where the zip-ties cut into the sides of his wrists.

Tears escaped the senator's eyes. He tried to look away, but Oliver turned his head back toward the action. He closed his eyes, and Ned punched him in the face.

"Pay attention, big shot. You're next," Ned said and laughed.

The senator thought of his wife and children. He hoped his wife was still paying the premiums on his life insurance policy. *They'll never let us live.*

Carl finished. "Paul, you wuss. Your turn. Do him," Carl ordered. He turned to Ned and Oliver and motioned them to the other end of the picnic table with the senator. "Do him," he yelled and then laughed as the senator struggled in vain. When all seven men were done, Ned taped the sheriff's mouth, and made sure the tape on the senator's mouth was still secure. Vince and Bert threw the sheriff and the senator to the ground. They all attacked, landing repeated kicks to the head, face, and body. After the bodies of the sheriff and senator no longer moved, the thugs stopped kicking.

"I hear a boat coming," said Carl Mitchell. "Just leave 'em. Let's get out of here. Let's ride!"

CHAPTER 8

The Agreement

Senator Billy's left eyelid slowly opened. The right one refused. *Where the hell am I?* He eased his right hand from underneath a sheet. It hurt to move. He felt pain coming from several areas. The fingers of his right hand carefully surveyed his right eye. It protruded from its normal location. It was swollen shut.

Then he remembered everything. "Oh, dear God in heaven, thank you, thank you. I'm alive. I'm still alive. I didn't think I would be." Tears formed in his eyes. *I just knew they would kill us. Am I okay? This must be the emergency room. Jack. Oh my God, is Jack dead? They probably killed him. I've got to find out and get to him, if he's alive, before he says anything.*

Senator Billy dragged himself from the bed. He stood, leaning over the bed on his elbows, trying to get a grip on himself and hoping the pain would ease up. He was dressed in only a tie-in-the-back hospital gown and non-slip, light-blue socks. The gown was tied behind his neck and nowhere else. His butt was in the air. Weakness and pain washed over him. Landing in a bedside chair, he took deep breaths. Sweat popped out on his forehead. He reached for the pink plastic ice pitcher. He flipped off the top and drank cold water from the side. He grimaced, noticing pain in his rectum. He stood again and decided he could walk.

"Wake up, Jack," Billy said, slapping him gently on the face. Billy had found Jack in the next examination room. Billy pulled the curtain completely closed behind him. He was relieved Jack was alive. Jack was connected to a heart monitor. *Looks normal to me.* Nervous that someone might walk in, Billy reached for Jack's water pitcher, removed the top, stuck in his hand, and splashed cold water on Jack's face.

"Come on, Jack, wake up!" Billy whispered with urgency. Jack moaned as he turned his head toward Billy. A nasty-looking black, blue, and purple line circled his neck. His right eye was swollen shut and only a sliver of the left eye peeked out.

"Can you hear me, Jack?"

"Yeah, I hear you," he managed to get out.

"Jack, I've been thinking about it. I don't want anyone to know we were raped. I know you're in law enforcement, but please, Jack, no one must ever know we were raped. Say you won't tell anyone. Do you agree, Jack? Do you understand what I'm saying? Say something."

"I promise, Billy. I will never tell a living soul. Now you."

"Jack, I promise to you and God, I will never tell anyone."

"No matter what happens, Billy. No matter what happens, what anybody says or does, no matter what changes, and no matter how many years go by. You still won't tell."

"I promise, Jack. I won't tell. What are we going to say happened?"

"We'll tell that when we got there, a couple of people hit us in the back of the head, knocked us out, and must have beaten us up after that. We didn't see them or hear them. That's all we know. Anything else they ask, we don't know. Got it?" Jack asked.

"Got it, we were just beaten up," Billy said. "Jack, I'm sorry I got you into this." He teared up.

"No, Billy, it's not your fault. It's mine. I didn't handle any of it like I should have. I knew better. I don't know what got into me, and I don't understand why I did what I did. I'm sorry. I could have done better."

"Jack, it's not your fault. Those that did this to us, they're to blame."

"Don't worry, Billy. I'll get them. They'll pay for what they did. Don't worry."

The curtain was jerked open. "I'm Doctor Osborne. I see you're both here. If you want to stay together and don't mind, I'll talk with you together. Otherwise, Senator, you'll have to go back to your room." Both nodded their approval. Billy pulled up a chair.

"I've looked over your x-rays. Both of you were beaten badly, but there's no need to keep you here. Sheriff, you've got three fractured ribs but not completely broken, no jagged edges. That's the good news. Yours are cracked, hairline fractures. They cannot be immobilized like a broken arm. They will heal on their own with time. It may be hard to take a deep breath, but you need to breathe as deeply as possible. You don't want to get pneumonia. The bad news is you're both going to be quite sore for a while. I have some discharge instructions and a prescription for each of you for the pain. The nurse will go over all that with you before you're discharged. You may both go home. You should make an appointment with your own physician next week if you don't see significant improvement in your situation. Sheriff, those ribs may take six weeks to heal. I don't have to tell you to take it easy. You're not going to want to move around much.

"Your families have been contacted and are in the waiting room. There's an officer who has been waiting to speak with you. I'll send him in to see you. Do you have any questions?"

Doctor Osborne quickly left, and Deputy Sheriff Mark Jenkins entered the room.

"Hey, Sheriff, you look pretty rough. You too, Senator Billy. I've never known anybody that could get the drop on you, Sheriff. Must have been more than one, for sure. I just came by to take your statement and to tell you we went over the crime scene and didn't find anything. The detectives were out of town for that training program you sent them to, but they'll go out there tomorrow morning to look over it, in case we missed something."

"I appreciate you coming by to let me know, Mark. It will be a short report for you. We got out of the car, took a few steps, and were both hit in the back of the head with something at the same time and were knocked out. Evidently, we were beaten after we were knocked out. That's it. That's all we know. We were ambushed."

"Thank you, Sheriff. I'll get that typed up and have it ready for you to sign when you're feeling well enough to come in. I'll tell the ladies outside y'all are ready for them."

CHAPTER 9

Max

Thank you, Sarah, for bringing me home. It's really nice of you, and I appreciate it," Sheriff Raymer said. He was glad to be home and in his favorite chair.

"Well, I couldn't let my children's father hitchhike home from the hospital. I'll bring you over a pot of homemade soup tomorrow. That will be easy for you to heat up and should last you awhile. It'll be better for you than ordering pizza. I notice you're looking a little pregnant." She smirked and patted his stomach as she headed for the door. He liked that they were still comfortable enough together, and she still claimed enough ownership of him, that she could touch his body without asking or even thinking about it.

"I didn't know I was showing. Too much beer, I suppose. I've been meaning to do better."

"I like what you've done to your house, Jack. It looks nice. Oh, I brought a sack of dog food for Max." She turned back to him. "I didn't know how much you had left and knew you couldn't go out for a while. I put some in his dish and put the rest of the sack on the counter, so you don't have to bend down to get it. I know you're sore. I filled up his water dish. I'll see you tomorrow."

"Goodbye, tell the kids I love them."

Sarah left, and the house was quiet again, except Max snacking from his plastic food dish in the other room. His metal tag bumped against the dish with every bite. Max came walking in, licking his lips.

"Hey, buddy. I see you were chummy with Sarah. Where's the loyalty? She feeds you, and you take right up with her. You know I'm your papa. There's no momma around here anymore." Max turned his head sideways, making the sheriff laugh, which hurt. Max rested his chin on the sheriff's knee, watched his face, and whined a little.

"I know, my face doesn't look the same, does it, boy? It's a real mess, all black and blue, and swollen. But it's me, Max." The sheriff rubbed Max's head. "They really messed me up." His voice broke. He wasn't thinking of his face anymore. He teared up, and leaned forward, shaking his head. His elbow was on the arm of his chair. His cracked ribs stopped him before his head could reach his waiting hand. Max stood, stepped up into the chair with his front paws, and pushed his face against the sheriff's cheek.

"You *do* love me," he whispered. He put his arms around Max, and all his pent-up emotions about being raped escaped his carefully guarded, tough-guy, Marine exterior. Max licked his neck and a few of the tears on his cheek. The sheriff cleared his throat, and then carefully blew his sore nose. "Boy, it's hard to get a deep breath with these ribs.

"What the hell is wrong with me, Max? I haven't cried since I was a little kid. But I've never felt like this before, not ever." Max dutifully stared into his eyes and seemed to feel his pain.

"That was the first time in my life anyone has ever been able to get the jump on me." He shook his head and wiped a tear from his cheek. "What they did to me, Max... I... I never imagined it was that way when women talked about getting raped. I've never felt so helpless, vulnerable...violated, and mad, all at once. I'm still mad. I hate every one of them. I told them I'd kill them, and I'm going to! If I have to go to prison and to hell, I'm going to kill them, Max!

"I've lost Sarah. Angelica will never want me now. They deserve better than me anyway. No one will want me. I expect I'm ruined forever, Max. Maybe you'll still have me, my best friend." Max licked the side of his face again.

Sarah had given Max, the German Shepherd puppy, to her husband for Christmas the first year after he retired from the Marines. She had been reading articles about therapy dogs, had attended meetings with other military wives and thought Jack might benefit from the company of a dog. Sarah had been right. Jack loved Max from the moment they met. Somehow, Max's innocence, loyalty, and unconditional love had broken through all the defensive layers Jack had put into place. Jack was on the floor playing with Max in a matter of minutes, and their relationship had grown stronger with time. Even with the help of Max, Sarah still divorced him. He didn't blame her. He knew he was the problem.

It's great that Sarah and I get along so well since the divorce. Not many ex-wives would bring their divorced husband home and help them out. Sarah was always a good woman and a good wife.

He thought about the Marines and the strong tradition they have of sending their best enlisted Marines to Officer Candidate School. They had sent him at the rank of staff ser-geant, an E-6. The Marines had taken good care of him through the years. He and the other officers who came up through the ranks were often called 'retreads' in the Marine Corps. He had retired as a major at just over twenty years. Now at forty-four years old, he had been at loose ends for a while and felt like he was starting all over. He couldn't claim he was settled since the divorce, but with this latest event, he felt shaken to the core.

Oh crap, Mark said the detectives are going to the crime scene tomorrow morning. I've got to go out there and make sure nothing is found. He knew it would hurt, but he had to go. He carefully pried himself from the chair.

He went on his motorcycle, thinking he would be less notice-able and harder to identify. He wore a black helmet with a full-face, tinted visor. He rode past the turn off, noticing yellow plastic tape draped across the entrance, but no sheriff's car or personnel were present. He turned around and went back. Well before the turn-off, he slowed down to a crawl to reduce the sound of the motorcycle. He pulled off the road and was careful to stay on the grass and leafy areas as he approached the entrance to the trail. There was enough slack in the yellow do-not-enter tape, that he was able to lift it over his head and enter.

Once through the gate, he stashed the motorcycle behind some wild shrubs and trees, atop woody debris, to keep from making tire tracks in the dirt. Before walking from the brush, grass, and pine straw onto the dirt, he slipped his feet into plastic bags with cardboard in the bottom and secured them around his legs to prevent shoe print tracks. The sheriff walked the entire crime scene, looking for any trace of evidence. There was no trash to be found, no zip-ties, no duct tape, bottles, or cans. There was nothing. The sheriff found tire tracks from the truck with the big Mud Gripper tires. He went to work obliter-ating them with a light-weight metal, flat-ended shovel he'd brought with him. He grunted with pain each time his movement exceeded the safe zone.

Carl's tooth shone in a pile of damp leaves near the root of a live oak tree. The sheriff gingerly squatted down for it, went to the river's edge, and threw it in. Then he raked over the area where Carl might have dripped blood and scattered leaves and pine straw over it. He turned to go, and his eyes landed on the picnic table. He teared up, and then anger washed over him. *Bastards! I'll get them.* He returned to his motorcycle, stowed everything in his backpack except the small shovel which he attached to the motorcycle, positioning it beneath a bungee cord.

Sitting on his motorcycle, hurting and trying to catch his breath, he knew the pain pill was rapidly wearing off. Still, he cranked his motorcycle with great care not to rev the engine. He watched from behind thick foliage, waiting for passing cars to be out of sight before easing the motorcycle under the yellow tape, quietly onto Riverside Road and back to his home.

Finally, home. He downed another pain pill and went to bed with Max by his side.

CHAPTER 10

Information

Sitting in his truck, Sheriff Raymer stared at the brown brick building, trying to decide if he would really go inside or not. *I may as well finish my coffee before I go in. There's no sense in letting it get cold while I'm inside.* He drank slower. After finishing his coffee, he needed to go to the men's room, so he got out of the truck. He'd come in the truck because it was easier to get in and out of than the car, but he still groaned with pain as he exited it.

"Hey, Jerry. I didn't expect to see you here," the sheriff said as he exited the bathroom in the foyer of the building. He was at the local Rape Crisis Center to see Betty Jackson, the director, who was also a counselor, and Jerry's wife.

"I retired last year, and Betty's got me volunteering here a few days a week. You look like you were hit by a Mack truck, Sheriff. What happened?" Jerry asked.

"I got hit by a Mack truck." They laughed. "No, just a little accident," the sheriff said.

"I sure would hate to see what a big accident looks like on you."

"What do you do here when you volunteer, Jerry?"

"I carry heavy boxes around mostly." He laughed. "Well, I do some public education and training. Sometimes, I do some counseling. You know I'm licensed and worked for the State Department of Mental Health before I retired." He lowered his voice. "Sometimes we have male victims who would rather have a male counselor, and Betty has me work with them."

"So, you do training. I wanted to ask Betty about some training for all the staff at the sheriff's office. Maybe you could both come."

"Yes, I think training would be a wonderful thing for your office. I'll talk with Betty about it, and she can call you to work out the date," Jerry said.

"Sounds good. Okay if I take a few pamphlets with me now?" the sheriff asked.

"Sure, we've got loads of them. I know, I carried them in here. There's a rack by the door. Take all you want."

Sheriff Raymer picked out a variety of pamphlets on rape, thinking of himself and Emma. Then he abruptly left, hoping no one had seen him come or go. He parked under a shade tree on the town square near his office but didn't go inside. He sat in his truck, reading the pamphlets.

"…rapists seek to degrade their victims, to have power and control over them, to humiliate and harm, or make them fear him. It isn't motivated by sexual desire. Sex is used as a weapon to dominate and hurt others."

The sheriff teared up. "I gotta pull myself together. I can't keep doing this," he said aloud. "Get your shit together, Raymer! Well, I'm not going into the office, still boohooing. I'll take another day off." He thought of Emma and wondered how she was doing. He decided to take her the brochures he had picked out.

❖❖❖

"Hi, Emma, may I come in?" the sheriff asked.

"Yes, come in," Emma said reluctantly and dreaded whatever he would say next. She motioned him into the living room. "Have a seat. You look worse than I do."

"I guess it's a hazard of the job. Emma, I'm sorry about the way I questioned you at the hospital. You didn't deserve that. I hope you can forgive me. I want you to know I believe you and everything you said." He sat on the soft cushion of the sofa, sank down into it, and stifled his groan of pain. He dreaded the moment he'd have to get back up.

"Thank you, Sheriff." Her eyes widened. She could hardly believe what she'd heard.

"I brought you some brochures from the Rape Crisis Center. If you ever want to talk, they're extremely helpful. The phone number is on the brochures. I read these, and I'm ashamed of the way I treated you. Some ladies feel guilty about being raped, wondering if they are somehow partly responsible or if they did or didn't do something to cause it. This brochure says, '...most rapists would have raped someone else if you hadn't been there. They're not interested in sexual gratification with a particular person. They intimidate and abuse because of their own deficiencies.'"

The sheriff saw Emma wiping tears. He reached out his weathered and scarred hand, laying it over hers, tiny, smooth, and pale. "I'm sorry," he said, and she smiled a little.

"It just comes out, a nerve gets touched, and I can't control my emotions. I never know when it's coming." She saw tears in the sheriff's eyes and one sliding down his freshly shaven, bruised cheek. Her eyes widened in surprise. "You know what I'm talking about, don't you?"

He nodded his head a bit, moved his gaze from the floor, and looked into her eyes. "I do," he muttered.

Emma stared at him, and then said, "Sheriff, did you find the men who raped me?"

His sarcastic mind whispered to himself, "Did I ever." He looked back to the floor, trying to control his emotions. Jack, as a Marine, had boxed up his empathy, locked it tightly away like treasure in a chest, hidden it behind the secret wall in the corner of the basement of his heart, and forgotten it ever existed. Brute force, aggression, and demanding expectation tempered only by obsessive, stoic self-discipline filled the vacuum. It had served him well in the Marines. In the presence of Emma, and their shared experience, empathy seemed to seep from its treasure chest like gas from a leaking valve, threatening to blow at any moment.

"You did, didn't you? Were they the ones who hurt you?"

"Emma, I might have found them. I need to ask you some more questions."

"Sure, anything to help you," she said. "I think about it all the time. I can't get it out of my head. I try to forget about it and move on, but I can't. I'm so afraid I might run into them on the street somewhere. I think about how they would know me, and I wouldn't know it's them right away. I think if I hear them talk, I would know it's them. I'm afraid they might take me again. I stay home most of the time because I'm afraid to go out, but they got my driver's license with my home address on it. I'm scared and nervous all the time. Please, I hope you get them, Sheriff."

"Tell me again, Emma, everything you remember." He

took out his note-pad and asked questions, recording information. He asked her to carefully think of the names she'd heard that night.

"Carl," she said. "He ordered everyone else around and was really mean. He's the one who whipped me with the belt and did the most beating on me."

"Did you hear other names?"

"Yes. Oliver, Ned, and Bert. There was a 'P' name. Oh, just a minute. I wrote the names on a list, every time I remembered one. I've got it in my room." She hurried to get it. "Okay, here it is. The others are Paul, Vince, and Dougie. That's all I remember hearing. If there were any more, I didn't hear their names."

"Emma," he lowered his voice, "did you count how many times they switched out... how many different men were with you?"

"I think it was seven. I'm almost certain. A couple of them did, you know, one area and not the other, but most did both areas."

"Thank you, Emma. I know it's tough to think about and talk about it again, but it's been very helpful to me."

"There's no one else I can talk to about it. It's not like anybody's gonna want to hear about this, not even a close friend. Maybe I do need to talk about it with the counselor."

"I'll go with you your first time if you need a little support, Emma, or a ride."

"Sheriff, these men I named, are they the same ones who hurt you?"

"Yes, Emma, but I need you not to tell anyone that, and don't tell anyone the names of the men. Each person you tell is likely to tell at least one other, if not more. We don't want word to get back to the men that you remember their names. Don't tell your parents, Noah, your friends, or anyone. Do you understand? Can you promise that for me?"

"Yes, I can do that. Just knowing you know who they are makes me feel so much better. But will we ever be able to win in a trial?"

"Don't worry, I'm going to get them. You don't have to be afraid. I'll see to them." He rose to go.

"Thank you very much for coming by, and for the brochures. I hope you'll come again."

"I hope you'll read the brochures, and you can stop by my office anytime. When will you go back to school?"

"Probably next Monday. I might still be a little bruised and sore, but my best friend told everyone I fell down a flight of stairs."

"Smart friend. Goodbye, and take good care, Emma," he said as he opened the front door.

"Sheriff," she called to him. He turned back to her. Emma moved to him and threw her arms around him in a hug. The tough Marine in him was stiff as a board, but after a moment, the part of him who now knew exactly how she felt, softened and relaxed into her warm hug. "Thank you… more than I can ever express, thank you," Emma said.

CHAPTER 11

Your Black Eye

"Billy, you sure got a lot of free publicity with your black eye." Sheriff Raymer laughed. "But I'm glad you took care of the reporters, so I didn't have to make a statement."

After Sheila at the sheriff's office called area television stations and newspaper reporters for a press conference, and the sheriff and Senator Billy didn't show up, the reporters wanted to know what happened.

Senator Billy went home from the hospital to rest, but his mind, in spite of his recent trauma, was always focused on publicity for re-election and building his platform for his future bid for governor. He knew he could parlay his unfortunate event into good fortune for his campaign, in his typical, 'make lemonade from lemons' positive fashion. The senator asked Sheila to reschedule the press conference for the following day. The press conference statement was the free publicity the sheriff mentioned.

The sheriff had stopped by Senator Billy's house to check on him and follow up on their last conversation in the hospital emergency room. His children were in school.

"Where's your better half, Billy?" Jack wondered if they were alone in the house.

"Sherry's with the church choral group. They're singing today over at Silver Pines Health Care for the senior citizens."

"That's where my grandfather lives. I hope he's in her audience. I'll ask him when I see him," Jack said.

"Want some coffee?" Billy asked, getting mugs without waiting for an answer. Jack sat at the small kitchen table as Billy poured the coffee.

"Are you all right, Billy?" Jack asked.

"I am. But every now and again, a wave of all that happened washes over me and… and it's overwhelming. It takes me a few minutes, and then I get myself together and move ahead," Billy said. "What about you, Jack? Are you all right?"

"Yeah, I'm fine."

"Don't give me that crap. I know you can't help but put up your tough guy front, you always have. But I want to know how you really are. I know you got everything worse than I did that day, and I know I'm more able to accept what happened and move on than you are. You know, I've never been in a fight my whole life. I got hit a few times and called 'momma's boy' more than once. So how are you really, buddy?" Billy asked, looking him square in the eyes.

"I don't hardly know how to describe it. I guess it washes over me too, but it stays awhile, going around and around in my head like a whirlpool. It feels like something inside of me snapped, and it's broken now. I sometimes feel like I'm not the same person as I was before. Sometimes I feel out of control. I can't always keep my emotions in check. I know that's stupid, but that's the way I feel."

Billy wanted to know how Jack was really doing, but he didn't know what to say when Jack actually told him.

"Jack, I'm going to look into all that stuff you told me about the rape kits not getting processed. There's a lot of things I can't do, but I can look into that and the other issues around rape. There may be some things I can do legislatively to help matters for everybody in our state who is touched by rape. I'll get started when I get back to Montgomery."

"Great, Billy. I hope you do. Of course, all that goes right along with your 'get tough on crime' platform you're trying to build." Jack laughed.

"I saw you on news broadcasts on three different stations," Jack said. "You were sporting your swollen black eye, talking about getting tough on crime, and telling how we were ambushed. I was the butt of a lot of jokes, thanks to you."

"Guess what?" Billy said. "My publicist sent that video clip out to every television station in the state, and they all played it. It didn't show on the same day everywhere, and it varied as to what time of the day it was shown, but it was everywhere. It made all sixty-seven counties. How great is that?"

"That's good, Billy. I know you'll be our next governor."

"That's my plan. Maybe all my publicity will be positive." Billy laughed.

"It's been a while now. Are you still committed to not telling anyone we were raped?"

"Absolutely. You're still on board, aren't you, Jack?"

"Yes, I am. There's one loose end."

"What do you mean? What are you talking about?" Billy's voice revealed panic.

"When we got to the emergency room, they cut our clothes off us. The hospital staff asked your wife and my ex-wife to bring clothes when they came to the hospital. A nurse told me it's routine to cut the clothes off when someone comes in like we were. I knew that, but you remember those thugs took our clothes off of us out there by the river. When we got to the hospital, we had on clothes."

"Oh my God, that's right. How could I not have thought about that?"

"You know the doctor didn't say anything about sexual assault. I think if there had been any blood around that area, there would have been something said about it. I'm glad, but I don't understand what happened. Remember the deputy who came in before we left the hospital? He said they went over the crime scene and didn't find anything. After I got home, I went back out there. There weren't any zip-ties, cans, or bottles."

"I can't believe you went anywhere the day we were released from the hospital. I could hardly move, and you were worse. Well, maybe those thugs who beat us did a cleanup and put our clothes back on us," Billy said.

"I don't see that happening. I checked who had called in the 911 report. It was the same name for us as it was for Emma, a man named Jake Dawsey. I'm going to see him. Maybe he can shed some light on it."

"So, if he's the one who put our clothes back on, then he knows we were raped," Senator Billy said with a worried look.

"There's no need to worry now, Billy. It's been a while and we've not heard a single thing about it. If he had told anyone, it would have spread over this whole county like a wild fire. I'll find out what happened and where his head's at when I see him."

"You don't think he's planning to blackmail me, do you?"

"Don't start imagining things. I'll go see him, and I'll find out."

"All right, Jack. But don't keep me waiting too long. Let me know as soon as you find out."

"I will. I better get back to work." They said their good-byes, and Billy walked Sheriff Raymer to his car.

CHAPTER 12

The DUI

Dadgum drunk drivers," said Sheriff Raymer. Driving home from an evening city council meeting, he was tired, still sore and hurting, and wishing he was already sitting in his comfy recliner. He usually attended the city council meeting because he worked closely with the city police on many projects. It was the last straw when the driver in front of him swerved into the oncoming lane. He flipped on his blue lights and siren. The car stopped, and he ran the license plate. "Well, I'll be." The tag check revealed the car to be registered to Emma's mother, Gayle Symner. He groaned getting out and walked to the driver's side window.

Emma's brother, Noah, peered up at him but quickly looked away. He handed the sheriff his driver's license and registration without looking up.

"Young man, step out of the car, please."

Noah stood, side-stepped to close the door, and leaned on the car.

"Do you know what the penalties are for driving under the influence in the state of Alabama?"

"Wait, you haven't tested me for that," Noah said.

"I know drunk driving when I see it. Do you want me to test you?"

Noah looked at the ground and slowly shook his head.

"A first-time DUI conviction can get you up to a year in jail or a fine ranging from $600 to $2,100 or both, plus license suspension and probation. Then you gotta pay to get your license reinstated, and your car insurance is going to be sky high. And I don't suppose you'd want to brag about your conviction on your college applications. What were you thinking about, getting behind the wheel, drunk? Not to mention where you got booze from at sixteen years old."

Noah wouldn't look at him.

"Noah, I know your family is going through a lot right now but drinking isn't going to help the situation."

"Yes, sir." Noah looked up at the sheriff and started to cry. "It's all my fault, what happened to Emma, it's my fault." His face was red, and his slight frame trembled as he folded his arms across his chest, hugging himself. He rocked from one foot to the other.

The sheriff reached out to put his hand on Noah's shoulder, and Noah lunged forward, putting his arms around the sheriff's waist and his head against the sheriff's chest, as he cried. With an automatic reflex, the sheriff raised his arms in front of him like a conductor directing a symphony. After a moment, he lowered them around Noah's shoulders and gently hugged him.

"Everything's going to be all right. You're going to get

through this," he said and then thought to himself, *I've had about all the tears I can handle.* He patted Noah on his back.

"Noah, come sit in my car for a minute. I want to talk with you."

Sitting in the car, Noah said, "I wish I could do something to find the men who hurt Emma."

"Well, that's just what I was thinking," said the sheriff. "I know you feel like a slug in a ditch and probably think you deserve to go to jail. But I've had a lot more experience in these matters than you, and I think your penalty should be serving some volunteer time. Be at the sheriff's office Saturday morning at nine o'clock."

"Really? Thank you, Sheriff. What will I be doing?"

"Emma told me both of you are into computers. So, you're going to be a volunteer computer forensics investigator, and you'll compile a list of names who will be leads for me as I track down bad guys."

"Wow, that's great." Noah smiled. "I'll be there on Saturday."

"Be on time. If you're late, you can scrub the toilets and mop the floors instead."

"I'll be on time. Do my parents have to know about my drinking?"

"You tell your parents whatever you see fit. That's between you and them this time, but I better not catch you drinking again."

"Thank you, Sheriff."

"There's one more thing, Noah. I want you to think about something. This business about who's to blame for what happened to Emma. You think it's your fault. The men who did it are the ones to blame. But you think you being late set it in motion, so you're blaming yourself. Right?"

"Yes, sir."

"Where were you anyway?"

"I was playing games at the arcade with my friend. A girl, Nancy, came over to talk to us. I've liked her a long time but haven't ever let her know. I could tell she was interested in me, and I wanted to stay longer to talk. It was so nice. I didn't want it to end. I asked her if she would like to go out with me sometime and she said, 'Yes.' I could hardly believe it," Noah said.

"That's great. You should ask her out even if it's for a walk in the park after school or to a ball game. It doesn't have to be fancy. She will appreciate it if she's the girl for you. All this with Emma has interfered with everyone's routines, but you've kept that girl waiting to hear from you all this time. Don't keep her waiting. Girls don't like that. You find her tomorrow and ask her for ice cream or something, anything. Oh, and hold her hand while you're walking."

Noah was smiling like the Cheshire cat. "Okay, I'll talk to her tomorrow."

"Noah, there were a lot of choices made that night Emma got hurt. You need to keep in mind that your choice was just one of them."

"I don't know what you mean, Sheriff."

"When you weren't on time, your mother chose to pitch a fit. She yelled at Emma about you being late. What if she had chosen to say nothing to Emma and, instead, taken it up with you when you got home?

"Emma chose to get between you and your mother and go looking for you. What if she had chosen to stay out of it, had told your mother she didn't know where you were, and left it right there?

"Out of all the places in this city Emma could have gone looking for you, she chose to leave the city and look for you in the woods. What if she hadn't chosen to go to the woods?

"Emma got to the woods and chose to jump out of the car and head toward the fire. What if she had sat in the car for just a minute and noticed that the people around the fire weren't you and your friends, had locked her doors, and gotten on the phone?

"There were a lot of choices made leading to what happened. Your choice to be late couldn't have caused this by itself. All those other choices had to be made. Can you see this isn't your fault and you aren't to blame, son? The people to blame are the ones who did it. They bear the full responsibility."

"Emma also told me, the ones who did it are the ones to blame."

"She's a smart girl. Believe it. Okay, let's get you home. I'm going to park your car in that parking lot across the street to get it off the roadside. Then I'll drive you home. You can come back for it tomorrow. Does that sound all right to you?"

"Yes sir. That'll be fine," said Noah.

CHAPTER 13

What If

Gayle stopped by Emma's room to check on her a while after they'd eaten supper. She found Emma sitting on the side of her bed in her nightgown.

"Going to bed, honey?"

"Momma, what if I'm pregnant?"

"Chances are you aren't. This was your first time. You were probably bleeding enough to wash things back out. Women don't usually get pregnant the first time," Gayle said, hoping it was true.

"But, Momma, what if I am? I just don't think I can carry the fetus of a rapist inside of me. I'll have to have an abortion, Momma. I just cannot stand the thoughts of having the genes of that kind of a vile, evil entity inside of me."

"Well, honey, the baby wouldn't be that way. It was the man who was so bad. The baby would probably be sweet and wonderful."

"Momma, if a baby comes, half of its DNA will come from a rapist. The baby could be just as evil and full of the devil as its father. Every time I'd see it, I'd think of those men raping me. Every time it would misbehave, I'd see those awful rapists in it. If it did something wrong, I'd want to beat it to death, knowing it has the genes of a rapist inside of it. I can't have such a thing inside of me, Momma. I will need an abortion."

"Now, Emma, you're just imagining things. You need to calm down. You're still upset about what happened to you. You're probably not pregnant.

"You know the law has changed, and it's against the law to have an abortion now. You know we fought to get that law changed, and you know why. But more importantly than man's laws, you know it's against God's commandments to kill another."

"Momma, abortion is the termination of a pregnancy, not a baby. It's not a person at conception; it's not a person until after the fetus is able to survive outside the womb after its birth. It's not a living human being because it's not alive. It's just a parasite living off me and sucking the blood and nutrients out of my body like a tape worm. It's not breathing on its own. It's not a person, so it cannot be murdered."

"Emma, where in the world did you come up with all that? You must have been on your computer to find stuff like that. You know good and well we don't believe that way. You know what we believe and what we have taught others. You know we believe it is alive and taking it would be murder."

"Momma, you don't understand. I know you don't. How could you? You've never been beaten and spoken to like a dog and gang-raped by seven drunk men."

"Emma, hush! You stop it, now. Stop talking about that. It's over and done with. You have to just move on with your life and forget all of it. I don't want to hear any more about it."

"You don't want to hear about it? You can't stand to hear

it. Well, it happened, Momma. It happened to me. You need to know. I should describe it, so you can better understand why I cannot just forget all about it, and why I cannot carry the seed of any of those men in my womb. If I am pregnant, I have to have an abortion, Momma. You've got to understand. Please, Momma, say you understand."

"No, Emma, I don't, and I will not understand that or accept that as being right in God's eyes. I know it's wrong. I cannot change my belief about this. You're just upset. If you're pregnant and don't think you can raise the child, then maybe your father and I will raise him or her."

"That'll be great, Momma, just lovely, having the product of my rape living here in this house. If it is here, I will not live here and will never come back here, ever again. You want to trade me in for the monster of a rapist?"

"Emma, get a hold of yourself. You don't know the child would be any sort of monster. You don't know what made those men into who and what they are. As a last resort, the baby could always be put up for adoption. There are lots of people who are barren and want to adopt babies. You're probably not pregnant, and we'll have to wait and see. But if a baby comes, you'll learn to love him or her. I know you will, and I'll love being a grandmother."

"Momma, you can believe differently. You can support me. You can help me. I need your help. I don't think I can get through a pregnancy by a rapist. Momma, please believe me, and choose me over your beliefs."

"I am not a baby killer. You remember those signs we made for the protests, and the anti-abortion rallies we did in front of those abortion clinics? We are not baby killers, Emma."

"You don't really love me at all, Momma. Get out!" She threw the red plastic cup she'd been drinking from, against the wall as hard as she could. Orange juice ran down the wall. Gayle gasped and fled the room.

Emma was shaking. She felt something new, which she decided must be rage. She walked back and forth in her room. She wanted to beat the wall, to kick it, to throw things, to scream. She managed to hold it inside. She marched back and forth in her room for the next half hour, with her brain spinning and replaying all they'd said and adding more to it. Slowing, ever so gradually, she finally stopped, sat on the side of her bed, and wept. After she'd cried all she could, she knelt beside her bed.

"Dear God. Help me, please. I don't know what to say. I just need your help. I know you know what's best for me and what I need. Please help me through all this. Please help me know what's right, what's the truth, and help me feel all right with whatever it is. God… you know everything, so you know my period is late. I know I've been through a lot and that might be why. I pray, please send it to me. Thank you. In thy name, Amen.

Please note: This book of fiction includes an imagined future time in which abortion has been made illegal. This is not factual information as of this book's published date.

CHAPTER 14

The River Rats

Sheriff Raymer stood behind a navy-blue van in the dark, waiting. Max whined softly. "Max, shh," the sheriff whispered and put his finger over his lips. They were outside the Swinging Oasis Club. A man approached. The sheriff listened to his steps on the gravel and stepped out in front of him, startling him.

"Dang, Sheriff, you nearly made me piss myself," Drake Steadman said.

"Howdy, Drake, I wanted to stop by to ask you a few questions."

The sheriff held up two fingers behind his back. Max moved closer and barked steadily.

"What's wrong with your dog, Sheriff? He's not fixin' to bite me, now is he?"

"Just stand real still, Drake. Don't make any sudden moves. Max here says you've got drugs on you."

"I believe I'm starting to not like dogs, Sheriff. Max might

71

have made a mistake. There must be something we can do to straighten this out."

"Max, sit." The sheriff replaced his two-finger command with an open-palm command. Max sat, stopped barking, and stared at the sheriff who, without taking his eyes off Drake, reached down with a treat for Max.

"I've been looking for some fellas. Maybe you know them and can help me out."

"I might can. Do you mind if we move over behind the van? No offense, but I don't want to be seen with you, Sheriff." Drake laughed.

"No offense taken. I might be bad for business, huh?" They moved a few steps over into the shadow cast by the van. "I'm looking for some badass thugs, seven of them who travel together. They're in their twenties, ride motorcycles, one of 'em drives a big muddy truck with Mud Gripper tires." The sheriff called off their names. "A guy named Carl seems to be in charge. What can you tell me about them?"

"I tell you what I know, and we're square, right?"

"As long as you know something worthwhile, Drake."

"Folks call them the River Rats, I guess because they usually hang out around the river and live around it. And they're rats, I suppose." He laughed.

"Why haven't I come up on them before?"

"Well, it might be because all of 'em except one guy live on the other side of the river in Georgia. There's one from over here, and I think he hasn't been with 'em all that long. They might have started coming over here after that guy took up with 'em."

"Where do they get their money?"

"They sell. They're my competition." He laughed.

"Which one is from Alabama?"

"It's the one who drives that truck you were talking about.

His name is Dougie Dinkins. I don't know the last names of the rest of 'em, but Dougie's been around here for a long time." Drake told the sheriff where he thought Dougie lived. "That guy, Carl, wears one of those German-style motorcycle helmets. Part of the time, he'll have on a black leather vest and sometimes a denim vest that says, 'Asshole' on the back of it. That about sums him up, too. He's mean and kind of crazy. Not 'I'm depressed' crazy, more like a frenzied, bug-eyed, on edge, manic kind of crazy. They all act like they're looking for a fight and if one guy gets in a fight, they all jump on whoever their guy is fighting. How about it, Sheriff, does that get me square with you?"

"Yep, that'll do it, Drake." The sheriff liked him. He knew Drake had a rough upbringing. Both of his parents drank and had been in and out of jail for drugs. He was twenty-one and had sold drugs from a young age but had never appeared to be using them himself.

"Drake, you're a smart guy. Smart enough that you haven't been arrested. You gotta know it's only a matter of time before you end up in prison. I know you had a hard time growing up, and you've done the best you could. You probably didn't have much choice in whether you were going to sell when you were twelve or thirteen, but you're old enough now that you can decide to do something else to make money. You can go out to the community college and learn a trade if you don't want to do the whole four-year thing. Or, you've had a lot of practical experience in running a business. You could get a business degree."

"Four years is a long time to go to school, Sheriff."

"Well, four years is nothing compared to how long you could end up in prison if you keep going like you are. I'd bet money you've got a gun on you right now. If you got into it with somebody and killed 'em, you could be in prison the rest of your life. But you can go to trade school for a couple of years and get started as an electrician or plumber, or whatever you want. They have a lot of things they teach out there."

"I don't know, Sheriff. A fella's gotta have money coming in to eat and pay the rent. I got a wife now and a baby on the way. I gotta have some cash flow."

"Most of your business goes on from noon to night, right? That leaves you free to go to school in the mornings. If I knew you were going to school and trying to do better, that would mean a lot to me, Drake. Think about it. What will your wife and baby do if you're in jail? Next term starts soon. You should talk to them out at the school."

"Thanks, Sheriff. I'll think about it. That's a good-looking dog you got there. I still don't like him though." Drake laughed as he walked away.

"Good boy, Maxie! Good boy." The sheriff gave him another treat. "Let's go home, Max. Let's go."

CHAPTER 15

Volunteer Investigator

"Good morning, Noah," Sheriff Raymer said. "I see you're right on time."

"Good Morning, Sheriff. I'm reporting for duty," Noah said with a smile.

"I see you're feeling better, young man."

"Yes, sir. I am."

"All right then. Come this way. I have a space set up for you." The sheriff led him down a barren-looking hallway with nothing on the walls. Shiny, waxed floors and institutional green walls led to the office where Noah would work. The room was equipped with a small desk that held a computer, printer, a legal pad of yellow writing paper, pens, and pencils. "How's this look to you, Noah?"

"I get my own desk? Wow, looks good," he said.

"All right, before we get started, there's one thing I need to know. Did you talk to the girl you're sweet on?"

Noah smiled broadly. "Yes, sir. I did just what you told

me to do. The way things are at home, I didn't ask her out for an evening. I asked her to the ice cream parlor for right after school, just like you said. We met out front of the school and walked there, so I held her hand. She smiled when I took her hand. We had strawberry sundaes and talked. It was really nice, and I got home on time too."

"Good for you. I'm proud of you."

"I am too," said Noah, still grinning. "That was my first date. Thanks for helping me get started. We had a great time."

"I know you want to help any way you can. I have a login set up for you for this computer. Your access will be limited to certain programs. You'll have a name badge to wear while you're here on the premises. Did they take your photo when you came in?"

"Yes, sir."

"Someone will bring it to you later. Whenever you're here, you will sign in at the desk, and they'll give you the name tag. When you leave, you turn it in and sign out."

"Yes, sir. I will."

The sheriff knew Noah needed something to do to help, to lessen his guilt.

"I have a list of five first names here. I'm interested in finding out their last names and where they live. I'm not going to talk with you about them or tell you anything about why I'm looking for them, so don't ask questions or assume anything about them. All I want you to do, is to put together a list of first and last names, and addresses. Is all that clear?"

"Yes, sir."

"In addition, all of this is confidential. You are not to talk about what you do here nor mention the list of names to anyone. If you happen to see someone else's work or over-hear someone's conversation while you're here, you're not to speak it to anyone. Understood?"

"Yes, sir."

"Here is your login and password, and an email account for you to use in relation to your work here. Here is a list of five first names. You can figure out where to look on the computer for information. You'll have access to the internet and social media and limited access to a few in-house programs. All of these names are the names of white males between twenty and thirty years of age. I suggest you start in the geographic area around River Rock and branch out. Do a separate page for each of the five first names. List the last name that goes with the first name, and then anything else you find about the person you think would be helpful in locating them. Questions?"

"No, sir."

"Here is the phone extension in my office. Call me a while before you're ready to go, and I'll come back. You can tell me how it's going and any thoughts you've had about it."

"Yes, sir. I will. Thank you again for letting me do this instead of arresting me."

"I appreciate your help, Noah."

CHAPTER 16

Dougie Dinkins

Sheriff Raymer knew he would recognize all the faces of the men from the clearing by the Muscogee River. He just needed to see them. He had already run the name of Carl Mitchell in his computer and was now running Douglas Dinkins. At the time, he didn't know if Carl Mitchell was the real name of the man he was talking to at the crime scene. The photo on Carl Mitchell's rap sheet matched the man the sheriff remembered. He was surprised because Carl had been so adamant about not producing his driver's license. The sheriff wondered why he'd used his real name.

Now that he had information on Douglas Dinkins, aka Dougie, he knew it wouldn't be long until he knew a lot more. He was sure of it and had been thinking about it ever since the rapes. Different scenarios took shape in his mind. He replayed all the possibilities again and again until a plan gelled in his mind.

❖❖❖

Looking through binoculars, the sheriff focused on the man

getting out of the truck at what he believed to be the residence of Dougie Dinkins. The sheriff sat on the back of his motorcycle across the road, behind some bushes on the edge of property planted in pines trees.

"Yep, that's him," Sheriff Raymer whispered.

Twenty minutes later, it was dark. The moon emerged from behind the clouds, giving enough light for the sheriff to make his way across the road to Dougie Dinkins' house. There were no outside lights burning. The sheriff eased up to a window. The curtain was not completely closed, allowing the sheriff to see Dougie sitting in a recliner, watching television and drinking from a can of beer.

The door handle turned in the sheriff's gloved hand. "Unlocked." He pushed gently against the door with his left shoulder. "No deadbolt." Gun drawn, he eased up behind Dougie Dinkins' easy chair. Vanna White touched and turned over letters as the sheriff simultaneously grabbed a handful of hair with one hand while putting the barrel of his pistol against Dougie's temple with the other.

"Move a muscle, and you're dead," the sheriff whispered. "Who else is here?"

"Nobody's here but me. What the hell? What's going on?"

"Lean forward and put your hands behind your back," the sheriff said calmly. Dougie still didn't know who was giving him instructions. The sheriff shifted the pistol to the back of his head. Dougie did as he was told.

"You make one sudden move, and you're dead. Got that?"

"Yeah."

The sheriff hit him in the back of the head with the butt of the pistol and handcuffed him.

"Damn, what'd you do that for? I did what you said."

❖❖❖

Sheriff Raymer took Dougie Dinkins outside.

"Where's your sheriff's car?" Dougie asked, looking around for it and other deputies.

"I don't have it with me, Dougie," the sheriff said. "Let's take your truck."

"You can't take my truck. What's wrong with you? You got to read me my rights and arrest me," Dougie said.

"Okay, Dougie, you're under arrest. You have the right to remain silent. Anything you say can and will be used against you in a court of law. You have the right to an attorney. If you cannot afford an attorney, one will be provided for you. Do you understand these rights I have explained to you?"

"Yes."

"With these rights in mind, do you wish to speak to me?"

"Well. Well, I don't want you to be mad with me. But I don't want to talk with you either."

"Suit yourself. Whatever you want to do is fine by me, Dougie."

The sheriff gagged Dougie and had him jump onto the tailgate of his own pickup truck. The sheriff pushed Dougie over onto his side and surprised him when he threw a pre-tied rope with a slip knot over one foot and quickly tied it to the other foot. Dougie's feet were tied to the handcuffs behind him. The sheriff drove to a secluded property by the river, owned by his eighty-five-year-old grandfather. The sheriff was the only one with a key to the lock on the gate. He usually visited the property to hunt or fish three or four times a year. He pulled up to the fence, got out, unlocked, and opened the gate. A sign on the gate read, 'Private Property, No Trespassing.'

After he entered and relocked the gate, the sheriff drove down the long trail. He passed his grandfather's rustic old hunting cabin. The entire property was fenced with the locked gate at the road.

The sheriff stopped the truck, got out, and lit up his portable LED camp lantern. He set the lantern on an upturned piece of log about three feet high and removed Dougie Dinkins from the bed of the truck. The sheriff seated him on a horizontal log laying on the edge of an old burn pit and removed the gag from his mouth. Dougie was facing the sheriff.

"What the hell are you doing?" Dougie Dinkins asked. "You're supposed to be taking me to the sheriff's office to book me into the county jail. What are we doing out here? This ain't right."

"What you all did wasn't right either. I have a few questions for you."

"I ain't saying nothing until I get a lawyer. The judge has

got to appoint me a lawyer. I ain't got to say nothing. You said so yourself."

"So now, you want to follow life's rules and proper legal procedure. I expect you're going to want to answer my questions," said the sheriff. "Now, I have all of your first names. You tell me everyone's last name. We can start with Oliver. What's his last name?" The sheriff took out his note pad from his breast pocket and turned it to the page where he had written all their first names.

"I ain't telling you nothing. And you can't make me. You have to wait until my lawyer gets here," Dougie Dinkins said.

"You don't seem to understand, Dougie. Your lawyer isn't coming out here."

"Well, well, you're going to have to take me to the county jail where my lawyer can come and see me."

"Again, you don't understand. I don't give a fuck about your lawyer. And we're not going anywhere until you tell me the last names of the others."

"But you can't do that. You're the sheriff. You have to follow the laws."

"You don't follow the laws, Dougie. You go around selling illegal drugs…"

"How do you know that?"

"Selling illegal drugs, raping and beating seventeen-year-old girls, and raping and beating me and the senator. If you don't follow the laws, then why should I?"

"But you have to," Dougie said, looking around and seeing nothing except trees and darkness.

"What is Oliver's last name?"

"I'm not telling. I'm not a snitch."

"I'm getting impatient with you, Dougie. Here's your last chance. What is Oliver's last name?" The sheriff pulled his 9mm Glock and pointed it at Dougie.

"You're just trying to scare me. You have to obey the laws. I ain't telling you shit."

The sheriff pointed the Glock and pulled the trigger, shattering Dougie's right knee cap. Dougie screamed in pain.

"What is Oliver's last name, Dougie? Do you want to lose your other knee too?"

"No, no, please. I'll tell you what you want to know."

The sheriff recorded the last names of all the other men, where they lived, where they hung out, and the name of the drug trafficker who delivered drugs to their gang to sell. Dougie confirmed what Drake Steadman had told the sheriff. All of the other men lived on the Georgia side of the river.

"I'm going to cut this rope. Now, stand up. Here, I'll help you. Turn around so I can take off your handcuffs."

Dougie Dinkins turned around with the sheriff's help. The sheriff removed the handcuffs. He pushed Dougie into the burn pit amongst logs, limbs, and debris, and shot him in the head, killing him instantly. He poured gasoline into the pit and threw in more logs and a match. Flames leapt into the air like a swarm of lightning bugs.

The sheriff opened a longneck bottle of beer, taken from his backpack, leaned back in his lawn chair, propping his feet on a log, and watched the fire burn.

Before getting back into Dougie's truck, the sheriff bagged his boots with Dollar Store bags from his backpack. He drove the truck back to Dougie's house, parked it, and left it unlocked with the keys in the ignition. The sheriff left the door to Dougie's house unlocked and open.

The sheriff walked across the road to his motorcycle and left. Back at his home, he put the gloves, the hair net he'd been wearing, and the Dollar Store bags into his fire place to burn. He cleaned his boots outside. He added the handcuffs to the washing machine with his clothes and turned it on. Then he got into the shower. Later, he dried and oiled his handcuffs and cleaned his Glock.

The sheriff left his holster belt and service weapon on the kitchen table and went to put away the 9mm Glock he'd used on Dougie Dinkins. Turning on the light, he moved to the left end of the carpeted, walk-in closet in his bedroom. On the inside of a storage cabinet, behind his Trauma Combat Medical kit, he flipped a hidden switch. The wooden panel wall to the side of the cabinet released. He pushed it open and walked through onto a landing at the top of a set of stairs. On the landing, against the wall stood the gun cabinet where he stored the 9mm Glock.

After he and Sarah divorced, he bought this modest-looking house because he thought it had what he needed to feel safe, secure, and ready for almost anything. The house was over a hundred years old. Parts of it had already been remodeled. Other areas had not been touched and needed work. Remodeling the house had been good therapy for him after the divorce, giving him something to think about and do, instead of feeling sorry for himself.

The downstairs basement, which was nearly as large as the house, was what sold him on it. After buying the house, he rewired it entirely and installed solar panels on the roof. He worked on the basement for the next few years, fortifying it with extra concrete and steel, and a ventilation system.

The basement contained an existing hand-dug, deep water well, over which the house was built. Having indoor water had been a luxury in the early 1900s. The well was surrounded by a circle of tightly fitted, interlaced, flat stones. A two-part hinged top had been added to keep animals and children from falling into the well. The front half of the top had a handle, allowing it to be raised and leaned backwards. A bucket could be lowered into the well to retrieve water. The back half of the lid nearest the corner wall was stationary. It had a hand pump built in on one side and on the other side a pipe extended to the upstairs kitchen where there was a second hand pump. Later, city water had been installed in the house, but the hand pumps and well were left intact.

The sheriff had added metal shelving in the basement, a small but complete second kitchen with appliances and several freezers all powered by solar. The shelves and freezers were stocked with two years of food, which he regularly rotated. He installed three other gun and ammunition cabinets, a medical cabinet, and added a bed.

Once his basement project was finished, he installed the secret passageway and closed off the original door going from the first-floor hallway to the basement. He took out the door and put a wall in its place. He had told no one about what he remodeled in the house and he'd had no house guests or visitors during his remodeling.

Having secured the Glock, the sheriff returned to his bedroom closet. He put the Combat Medical kit back in front of the hiding place for the release switch.

He first used the medical kits in combat situations while in the Marines. Aside from this one, he had one in his truck, his car, and his patrol car. It had most of the standard medical supplies used in emergencies. He bought the supplies separately and packed them himself, so he would know exactly what was in the kit and the exact location of each item to prevent time loss in the event of an emergency. A few of the many items in his pack were tourniquets, skin staplers, gauze, tape, bandages, ice packs, leg splints, gloves, masks, trach tubes, blood pressure cuff, stethoscope, pen light, sutures, aspirin, safety pins, hand sanitizer, eye pads, and butterfly strips.

The next day, the sheriff returned to the burn pit. He removed ashes, dirt, and bone shards into buckets. He carried them down the river in his boat and emptied his buckets. Farther down the river, he tossed his two spent shell casings.

CHAPTER 17

Old Jake

The sheriff pulled in at Jake Dawsey's address. He had called ahead, telling Mr. Dawsey he wanted to talk with him at his home. Mr. Dawsey was sitting on the front porch when he saw the sheriff and walked out onto the lawn.

"Howdy, Sheriff. Feeling better, I hope."

"I am better, Mr. Dawsey. Would you mind me asking you a few questions?"

"No, sir, I don't mind. Come on in. Everybody 'round here calls me Old Jake. You may as well too. I got hot coffee in there on the stove if you want some."

Old Jake's little wooden house was across the road and about a hundred yards south of the dirt trail turn-off to the place by the river that the teenagers called "the playground." The sheriff now thought of it as "the crime scene." The small house had tiny but tidy rooms. They walked through the living room to the kitchen and dining table. The sheriff placed a big paper bag on the table as Old Jake put out coffee cups and started pouring coffee from a stove top percolator coffee pot.

"I noticed on some paperwork, you were the one who called 911 when I got hurt across the road. I brought you a little something, a token of appreciation. I wanted to say thank you. When you told me on the phone you live by yourself, I thought you might be like me. I like to pick up cooked food sometimes, instead of cooking at home. Well, I guess I do that most of the time. It's an apple pie, a quart of barbecue pork, some sauce, and a pint of potato salad."

"Lawd, Lawd, that's some of my favorite things. I can't remember the last time I had any of 'em. Thank you, Sheriff."

"You're very welcome, Jake. I hope you enjoy them." Old Jake cut the pie and put a slice on a saucer for each of them.

"Sheriff, I don't mean any harm, but you still look mighty bad," Old Jake said.

"No harm done. I still groan just about every time I move. I've got some cracked ribs." The sheriff laughed a little. "Jake, I noticed you also called in the attack on the young girl that happened across the road. How did you happen up on her, and Senator Billy and me?"

"Well, a few years back, I got to noticing cars and trucks coming and going up there. Sometimes it was during the day, sometimes night. I first walked up there one day because I was curious to see what might be drawing the people. After dark sometimes, I would sit out there on my front porch, watching them come and go. My Social Security check each month isn't much, so I started walking up there each day to see what was left behind from the night before. I picked up cans and bottles and when I had enough, I took them to the recycling center. I never got too much, but it helped a bit. Those kids sometimes made a mess, so I picked up the trash too. After a while, I decided to put a garbage can up there, just like you would see in a park. I chained it to a tree with a lock on it and put in a garbage bag. Sometimes they put stuff in it.

"When that girl got hurt, I heard motorcycles roaring out of there that night, early, so I went up there before breakfast the next morning. That's when I found that poor little girl. I thought she was dead. It broke my heart to see her laying there like that, with dried blood all in her long, blonde hair. I just knew she was dead, she was so pale and white. I couldn't see a bit of color in her cheeks, but I checked on the side of her neck for a pulse, and she was alive. That's the only place I touched her.

"Before he passed, my son gave me this little flip phone when he got a snazzy new one. I called 911. I was a little scared to call. I was afraid she might die before she could tell them I didn't do it. The ambulance and police came. I went back out to the road to flag them down. I knew they'd never find where to turn in if I didn't. I told the deputy where I touched her.

"On the day you got hurt, I was sitting out there on the front porch. I heard, and then watched, those motorcycles leaving again, real fast this time. After finding the girl, I decided to go over there right away. And that's how I found you."

"I'm glad you found all of us so fast and got us some help," said the sheriff. "I wondered though, what made you put Senator Billy's and my clothes back on when you didn't dress the girl?"

Old Jake got up, took a big pot from the dish drain board, and put it on the floor in the living room. It had begun to rain. Water came through the roof, dripping into the living room. He set their empty saucers in the sink and poured them more coffee.

"I noticed your uniform and name badge laying in the dirt. I couldn't tell who you were by your face. It was a mess. I recognized the senator. He wasn't as bad. I could see what had happened to y'all, a shameful, sick thing. I didn't think you'd want anybody to know. So, I cleaned and dressed you. I found a piece of a roll of paper towel in the trash can and used river water. I figured if you wanted to tell, you could, but thought you should get to decide. Of course, I had to cut those ties on your hands and the senator's. Otherwise, I couldn't put your shirts on y'all.

"Many years ago, you were in high school and were the quarterback on the football team. You might not remember it but my son, John Dawsey, was on the team with you. He was younger than you, fifteen at the time. Times were precarious for black men, sometimes it still is. But four of the white players had been giving my son a hard time. They were roughing him up in the locker room one day and you came in and defended him. You stopped those other white boys."

"I remember John. He was our tall, skinny kicker, and was good at it."

"My son said you pushed the biggest of those boys up against a locker and called them all big bullies, as all four of them were seniors picking on one scrawny fifteen-year-old. You asked them couldn't they see he was scared and told them to have a heart. Then you told them, better yet, they should grow a brain. You told them, y'all were on the same team and had to work together, and he was the best kicker y'all had, and nobody should be beating him up. I don't know what else you might have said or done, but they never bothered him again.

"He got a scholarship to college as a kicker. If you hadn't defended him, he was going to quit the team, and he couldn't have gone to college. You protected my son. You never knew I existed until now, but all these years, I've remembered you, and I've known that I'd do most anything for you, Sheriff. Anything. Until then, all I could do was vote for you, which I've done twice."

"Thank you, Jake. I didn't know John got a scholarship. I joined the Marines after graduation that year and lost touch with what was going on back here with the team. I really appreciate what you did for me. What happened in the woods over there… it's a hard thing for a man to deal with, and I'm hoping you won't talk about it to anyone."

"Sheriff Raymer, you have my word. I'll never speak of it unless you have a reason and ask me to speak it."

"Thank you again, Jake. That takes a weight off my mind. Just curious… you didn't dress the girl?"

"Sheriff, I was afraid to even touch her to see if she was alive. I'm a black man, and I couldn't get away from her fast enough. If anybody had walked up, they would have seen a black man standing over a naked white girl. If she had died… well, you can imagine."

"Jake, what about the tape, zip-ties, bottles and cans that were out there on those nights? Do you know what might have happened to them?"

"Yes, sir. I went on and picked up out there. I saved those bags. You want 'em?"

"Yes, I'll take those with me." Old Jake went to a storage shed in back of his house and handed two garbage bags to the sheriff.

The sheriff took the bags, shook hands with Old Jake, and left.

CHAPTER 18

The Outing

Noah, would you do me a favor?" Emma asked. She knew he would. Her brother still felt guilty about her attack and frequently asked her if she needed anything. He'd never been so nice to her. Emma knew it wasn't his fault and was upset each time her mother chastised Noah for anything and threw in, 'It wouldn't have happened if you'd been where you were supposed to be!'

"Sure, Emma, anything," Noah said. He smiled and seemed so happy, Emma almost felt she was taking advantage of him. But she really needed him now.

She took his wrist, pulled him into her room, and closed the door. "Will you go with me to Sulphur Springs while Momma and Daddy are at church? I don't want to go by myself."

"Sure I will, Emma. I'll drive you."

"Noah, I don't want you getting caught between me and Momma if there's a fight about it later. I should tell you what I'm planning to buy. I'm buying it there because I don't want anyone in River Rock to see me buying it. I'm getting a pregnancy test."

"Oh, Em, I'm sorry you even have to wonder."

"I'm late," she said. "I may as well bite the bullet and find out."

"We can leave right after they do. We'll have plenty of time. Maybe it'll be good news," Noah said.

"Don't be nervous, Emma. It'll be okay."

"I don't think I can turn it off until I know I'm not pregnant."

"I can understand that. What'll happen if you are?"

"I don't know, Noah. I only know I don't want to have it."

Noah turned off the highway at the Sulphur Springs Health and Beauty. "Do you think they'll have it here?" Noah asked.

"I don't know, but most of the others look closed. They probably only open in the afternoon, after church lets out."

Noah parked and started getting out.

"Noah, I'll go by myself. There's no need in both of us being embarrassed."

"Are you sure, Emma? I don't mind going in with you."

"It's okay. I'll go by myself. Is there anything you want? I'll get us a soda and a snack of some kind."

Emma meandered around the store with her shopping cart. She picked up a Dr. Pepper and a Coke, a bag of jalapeno-flavored chips, and some cheese dip. She realized she was starving. *Why am I so hungry?*

She looked around and didn't see anyone she knew: a mother with a screaming two-year-old, an elderly woman at the end of the aisle looking at eye glasses for reading, a rough-looking guy in a denim vest in need of a shave, and a teenage couple looking at condoms. She quickly reached for the pregnancy test, then for a second one. She tucked them under her bag of jalapeno-flavored chips. She paid the cashier and was relieved to be leaving the store.

Emma stopped by one of the large columns outside, slipped the plastic bag over her wrist, and opened her purse to put away her change.

Carl Mitchell, dressed in a denim vest, saw her inside. He noticed the aisle on which she was shopping. He watched as she put two boxes in her cart. After she turned to check out, he followed up the aisle to see what the boxes were.

Emma had just zipped her purse when someone bumped into her from behind. Carl Mitchell was behind her. His body pushed up against hers. His arms were around her. He pushed her up against the column. She couldn't move.

"Don't make a sound," his deep voice ordered. She was transported back to the night of the rape. She froze. She couldn't think. She couldn't move. She couldn't have made a sound if she had tried.

"Are we having a little baby together, sweetheart? My rich bitch blonde cheerleader and momma to be?"

Emma was jolted back. She finally managed a deep breath and screamed for her life. "Shut up, bitch!" Carl growled. He looked around. Emma caught another breath and was on her second scream. People were looking. One of the teenagers who had bought condoms, started recording the scene on his phone. Emma was terrified but felt rage flying up from deep inside. She managed to turn and slapped Carl across the face with all her might, and then curled her fingers, raking her fingernails down the side of his face as she retracted her hand.

Carl reached to his back pocket and grabbed his red

bandana. It was tied to a heavy metal padlock. He swung it around hitting Emma in the eye with the metal padlock. "I know where you live bitch!" Carl yelled at Emma. He turned and swung again hitting the teenager in the head at his temple. Carl grabbed the teenager's phone and ran. Emma and the teenage boy both fell to the sidewalk. By the time Emma looked up, she only saw his denim vest over jeans rounding the corner.

"Emma, Emma, are you all right? What's wrong? What happened?" Noah asked as he ran to her.

A crowd formed around them. A loud motorcycle went speeding by.

"Do you want me to call the police?" someone asked.

"No," Emma said. "Noah, get me out of here! Noah, get me out of here, please!"

He got her up, put his right arm around her and took hold of her left wrist, leading her through the small crowd, as each told the next what they had seen and heard. The teenage boy lay on the sidewalk not moving.

In the car with the doors locked, Noah tried again, "Emma, what happened back there?" She told him what happened, begged him to drive, to get her home.

"Don't you think we should report it to the police? The store might have a video recorder somewhere. If we wait, it might be recorded over."

Emma sobbed. "Please take me home. Please take me home."

"All right, Emma. You're safe now. We're going home."

CHAPTER 19

I Don't Know What to Do

Emma asked her best friend Hayden to come over after school on Monday. After her encounter with Carl Mitchell at the Sulphur Springs Health and Beauty store, Emma had been so upset that she didn't use the pregnancy test she'd bought.

"If I thought I might be pregnant, I don't think I would have been able to wait to do the test," Hayden said. "I would have done it as soon as I got home from the store."

"I didn't tell you what happened at the store," Emma said. She told Hayden what Carl Mitchell had done and what he had said to her. "I was so upset that when I got home, I took one of the pain pills the doctor prescribed. It made me sleepy, which is what I was counting on. I went to bed and didn't get back up until this morning to get ready for school."

"Oh, Emma, no. It's awful what happened, and I know it's difficult, but you don't need to be taking pain pills to escape. There are other ways to cope."

"I know. I shouldn't have, but I just didn't feel like I could face anything more. I needed to get away and not think about any of it for a little while. I didn't want to think about Carl, the rapist, or the possibility of being pregnant, and most of all, I didn't want to think about the possibility of being pregnant with Carl's little parasite."

"So, that's why your eye is black. Did you report what happened to the police in Sulphur Springs?"

"No, I wanted to get home right away and made Noah bring me right then. He wanted to go to the police. I thought I had enough makeup on to cover up the bruise."

"Are you going to tell Sheriff Raymer about it? Maybe he could check into it."

"I am thinking about going to see him tomorrow after school."

"So, are you going to do the pregnancy test today?" Hayden asked.

"Yes, I am. I want to do it while you're here with me."

Emma opened her bedroom door and walked down the hall and back. "I don't see anyone out there." She closed the door. "I hid them in the closet." She went to her closet, pulled out a small trunk from the back corner, took a tiny key from the dresser, and opened it. She pulled out the plastic bag containing the pregnancy tests and handed it to Hayden.

"I can't bring myself to read all of that. You get to tell me how to do it."

Hayden pulled out one of the two boxes, opened it, and read the instructions to herself. She removed the plastic wrapper. "You have to pee on this plastic stick. Take this plastic top off the end of the stick, place the absorbent tip in your urine stream to get it wet, recap the stick, and then we wait."

"How long does it take?"

"After you recap, you come back in here and hand it to me, your loyal assistant, and then I'll tell you," Hayden said. "So, go already. Let's get it over with and move on with our lives."

"Oh, that sounds good." She headed off to the bathroom and returned quickly.

"What are you looking for?" Emma asked.

"In this little window pane, one line forms to show you it's working or that it got wet. If another one forms, you're pregnant."

"Let me see... no, I don't want to watch. I can't stand it."

Emma saw it on Hayden's face. "Your face, oh no, oh no!" She put her hands over her cheeks. "What am I going to do?"

"I'm so sorry, Emma."

Emma knew it was coming and wasn't shocked.

"What are you going to do? Are you going to tell your mother?"

"Not today. At my best, I can only handle one trauma per day. I had one yesterday, one today, and cannot deal with her today. I certainly am not at my best."

"She knows this isn't your fault, Emma. She'll understand, won't she?"

"I talked with her before. I knew I was late and suspected I might be pregnant. I told her I wanted an abortion if I am. We had an out-and-out war in here. I guess it was mostly me. She was fairly nice about explaining why it's not possible. I wasn't as nice about telling her why I had to have one."

"But she understands why you want one, doesn't she?"

"Hayden, my mother will never understand why I feel like I cannot have this fetus of a rapist inside of me. Momma has always been a pro-life advocate. She attended rallies and gave speeches about it all the time, back before the abortion laws were changed. She told me how she and Daddy might raise the baby, how I would love it, or that it could be put up for adoption.

"You know, I grew up in church and attended the anti-abortion rallies with her. I was one of those little seven-year-old kids you see on the evening news carrying a picket sign outside of an abortion clinic, saying what I was told to say. I didn't think about it. I was told it was wrong, so I believed what I was told. But now, I'm all torn up inside about it because I cannot stand the thought of having a rapist's fetus inside me. I'm not sure what I believe anymore. I just know I cannot have Carl, the rapist's, baby."

"What can I do to help you?" Hayden asked.

"I don't know if there is anything that will help me, but if there is, I need to find it. Could you help me find a place to have an abortion? Maybe you could call some places and give a fake name to ask about the possibility of an abortion. I'll do the same here. I wonder if there would be anything online about getting one."

"Emma, you better stay away from those online places. You can't tell whether it's someone for real who knows what they're doing, or if they are just going to rob you when you get there. And I've heard awful things about girls, years ago, who would go to places and be mutilated. Sometimes there was no anesthesia, and people said the places were filthy and girls got horrible infections. You have to be careful."

"That's scary stuff. What am I going to do?"

"I confess that I read online about abortions after you told me you got raped. I was curious. I read that if you're going to have an abortion, the earlier, the better. In the first twelve weeks is best. What about your daddy? I wonder if he might know someone who knows someone else who does them on the sly."

"I don't know, Hayden. He knows a lot of people. All of this about the rape has been tough on him, I think. He won't say anything, but I can tell. He's had a hard time looking me in the eyes since it happened. I hurt for him. I don't know whether he would be capable of getting words like that out of his mouth to ask someone. You can let me know if you think of anything."

"I will. I've got to get home. I'll see you tomorrow at school."

CHAPTER 20

Help Me, Sheriff

Ready, Emma?" Noah had been sticking close to Emma ever since the trip to Sulphur Springs. Emma was glad because she didn't want to go anywhere alone anymore. Noah volunteered to drive Emma, after school, to the sheriff's office to talk about what happened at Sulphur Springs. She wanted to talk to the sheriff alone, so Noah said he would work on his volunteer project while they talked.

"Yes, I'm ready." Emma waved goodbye to Hayden. She had walked with Emma from the school building through the parking lot to meet Noah.

Noah headed to downtown River Rock. Emma noticed the beautiful trees and flowers in the town square and wondered if she would ever be comfortable walking in the woods again. Then Emma caught a glimpse of the beautiful maiden standing in the fountain, looking to the sky with her arms raised. She thought, *Maybe she's reaching out to God, the angels, or others in heaven for help. She might be asking*

God to take her away from this world to heaven. Wouldn't that solve my problems? Noah parked and walked her inside.

"Hi, Noah." The pretty receptionist recognized him, and he smiled. She gave him his ID badge, and he signed in.

"Wow, Noah, a name tag. You're official." Emma was impressed.

The receptionist called the sheriff. Noah volunteered and was allowed to escort Emma to the sheriff's office. Noah asked the sheriff to call him to collect Emma when they were finished.

"Is it all right for me to close this door, Sheriff?"

"Yes, if you want to, feel free." She closed the door and then walked around the perimeter of his office, looking at everything. One wall had 8" x 10" photos of his Marine years. She noticed a photo of the sheriff wearing his dress uniform with his wife, Sarah. Another showed him in a combat uniform with his troops. There were a couple of photos of his children, sitting on the credenza running along the left side of his desk. The chairs were leather and big. They matched the masculine sofa against the wall, which was near a round table for small meetings.

"Where was this picture taken? The one with you and the soldiers," Emma asked. "That was taken with my troops in Afghanistan during the war."

"Y'all were fighting and killing people?"

"It was war, Emma. That's what happens when troops serve their country during wartime.

"Yes, I suppose so."

"Are you here for an update, Emma?"

"No, Sheriff. I came to update you."

"Well, has something happened?"

"On Sunday, Noah drove me to Sulphur Springs Health

and Beauty Store. I bought a pregnancy test there. I'm pregnant, by the way."

Sheriff Raymer raised his hand to his heart. His face turned pale. "I'm sorry, Emma. I'm very sorry."

"Me too. When I went outside, that thug ring leader who raped me grabbed me from behind, pushed me up against a column, and talked about me and him having a baby together. He must have seen me inside and saw what I bought. I saw him inside but didn't know it was him until that happened outside."

"What made you know it was him?"

"He used some of the same words he used that night in the woods. He said, 'Are we having a little baby together, sweetheart? My rich bitch blonde cheerleader and momma to be?' And his voice was the same."

"What else do you remember?"

Emma told him about her screaming, slapping and scratching Carl, about the bandana and then Carl running away. She told him she had seen on the back of his denim vest the word, "Asshole."

"Did you call the police in Sulphur Springs?"

"No, I was a wreck. I made poor Noah bring me home. He wanted us to go to the police, but I wouldn't. I decided I'd better tell you. I'm afraid to go anywhere by myself."

"It's best right now to have someone with you all the time, just because it will make you feel better, feel safer, and it will deter anyone from approaching you like that. I want you to know, I'm following some leads and I will get them. There will come a day when you will feel safe again and will know you don't have to be afraid of them anymore. I promise you that."

"Thank you, Sheriff. That will be a fine day and it can't get here fast enough for me. I need help with one other thing. I don't know who to talk with about it."

"What is it, Emma?"

"I cannot carry Carl's fetus around in my body, and I will not bear his baby. Please, I need an abortion. Please help me find a place to get one."

"Does anyone else know you're pregnant, Emma?"

"I haven't told Noah or anyone else. The only person who knows is my friend Hayden. She was there with me when I did the test. She won't tell anyone, if that's what you're worried about. I could even tell her I miscarried or something. Please help me."

The sheriff sat, staring out the window with his chin on his fist.

"No one would know that you helped me. Please," Emma pleaded.

"Emma, you know all of the abortion clinics were shut down, that abortion is illegal now, and I am sworn to uphold the laws. I'm deeply sorry you're pregnant. I'll help you in any other legal way I can. I'll drive you to see Betty Jackson at the Rape Crisis Center, if you want. I'll get the rapists. But I can't help you get an abortion."

"It's not enough I get raped, but then the laws keep me from getting the morning-after pill and now I'm pregnant. The laws have added victim punishment to the rape. If I find a place to get an abortion, then you can arrest me, and I'll be a criminal too." Emma turned and stormed out.

CHAPTER 21

We Meet Again

For four evenings, Sheriff Raymer had been watching the rundown mobile home where Carl Mitchell lived. He wanted to know about Carl's coming and going patterns. If Carl stuck to the routine the sheriff had witnessed for the last three days, he should be arriving home any minute. The sheriff smiled when he heard the loud motorcycle approaching.

"Tonight's the night," said Sheriff Raymer. He knew Carl would likely be home about an hour before leaving again. He reviewed his plan in his head, step by step. As the minutes passed, the orange sun slipped below the horizon, and darkness crept from the cervices like a black fog devouring the light. The sheriff moved to his truck, tucked into a row of large trees, where he had parked. Now he was ready to emerge from the field road. His truck windows were down. He heard the motorcycle taking off. His heart beat slightly faster. The motorcycle neared at a high rate of speed. The sheriff calculated, waited, and floored it, springing the truck out onto the road at the exact right moment. Carl Mitchell put on the brakes and swerved left to keep from crashing into the truck. The motorcycle fell to the left and went skidding into the ditch. Carl jumped up and headed back to the truck, cursing.

"You damn son of a bitch, where the hell did you get your license to drive?" Just as Carl neared the truck, Sheriff Raymer stepped out with the 9mm Glock drawn.

"Hands on your head, Carl. Now!"

"What are you doing in Georgia, Sheriff? You're off your beat by a whole state."

The sheriff pushed him up against the truck and hand-cuffed him.

"You got no jurisdiction over here, Sheriff. Who do you think you are? You still think you're some kind of big shot, huh? I thought I corrected that notion for you a while back. Maybe you came back for some more. Maybe you liked it." Carl laughed.

The sheriff tore off a piece of duct tape and put it over Carl's mouth. "There now, that sounds much better." He ordered Carl into the back of the truck by way of the tailgate. When Carl didn't move, the sheriff punched him in the gut and then pushed him up onto the tailgate. He reached for rope he had prepared ahead of time. He slipped it over one foot, pulled it tight, and quickly wrapped and tied the other foot with it, like wrestling a steer in a rodeo. Then he looped the rope through the handcuffs, pulled tight, and tied it off. Carl's feet were pulled backwards toward his hands. The sheriff jumped into the bed of the truck and dragged Carl to the front, behind the cab, by his shirt collar. He covered him with a blue tarpaulin.

"If you move around or make any noise, I'll kill you. You got that?"

The sheriff moved the gas can to the rear of the truck and raised the tailgate. He had to stop for gasoline for the can. In spite of all his planning, taking Carl today had been a spur of the moment decision. He'd thought of Carl accosting Emma outside the store in Sulphur Springs and was livid, knowing that if Carl got the chance, he'd do it again. He couldn't bear the thought of Emma going through that again.

The sheriff pulled into a gas station near his home on the Alabama side of the Muscogee River, even though it was out of his way when going to the hunting cabin property. He didn't want to be seen getting gas for the can anywhere else.

"Hey, Sheriff, how are you?" Rodger Davis, from just down the road, was filling up his tank on the other side of the pumps.

"I'm great, Rodger. How about you?"

"I'm fine. You cutting grass tomorrow, Sheriff?"

"We wouldn't know it's Saturday if we weren't cutting the grass, would we?"

"You got that right," Rodger said.

The sheriff put his can of gas back in the truck. Carl started making sounds, trying to get Rodger's attention. He got louder.

"You better shut up, boy," the sheriff said in a low growl. Carl made an even louder sound. The sheriff picked up a tire iron and hit him in the head, through the tarp.

"Are you all right over there, Sheriff?" Rodger asked.

"Yeah, I'm fine. I just caught my hand on a piece of metal while I was tying up this gas can, is all. It'll be fine. Seems like the older I get, the more prone I am to catching some part of me on something every day."

"I know that's right. I do the same thing. See you later,

Sheriff." Rodger drove away, and the sheriff walked over to the sliding window to pay cash for his gas.

The sheriff poured gasoline into the bottom of the fire pit. He had sunk a wooden post earlier, positioning it just outside of the burn pit on the far side. The sheriff wanted his handcuffs back. Carl was still out of it from the tire iron blow to his head. The sheriff removed the handcuffs and tied Carl's hands in front of him with rope at his wrists. He put a rope over Carl's head around his neck, pulled it tight, and suddenly flashed back to Carl choking him with his belt during the rape. He pulled Carl by his wrists, dragging him to the other side, and dropped him into the edge of the pit. The sheriff tied the rope around Carl's neck securely to the post. Carl's back was against the side of the burn pit.

The sheriff returned to the other side and sat in a lawn chair facing Carl. The sheriff noticed the wind had picked up. He checked the sky. The wind and clouds were moving away from him, across the pit, toward Carl. It wasn't black dark yet, but with full cloud cover, he knew it would be soon. The wind was taking care of the gas fumes from the pit. Even so, he moved away from the pit to open his LED camp lantern before returning. *No sparks.* He positioned it on top of the cab of his truck.

Earlier, he had left a little cooler beside his chair. He reached in for a longneck bottle of beer, took a long slow swallow, and set the bottle on the flat-top stump next to his chair which made a fine side table.

With Carl gone, the others won't have anyone telling them what to do, and they sure as hell won't know what to do.

The sheriff felt nothing, certainly no empathy for Carl Mitchell. While each function and task he'd performed was done almost perfunctorily, he did care passionately about fulfilling his mission. He proceeded methodically toward his ultimate goal: the annihilation of his enemy and Emma's tormentors, and the consummation of his sworn revenge.

Carl Mitchell was coming to. The sheriff twirled a long kitchen match from one finger to the next. A box of them sat on the stump next to his beer.

"No wonder you didn't want me to see your driver's license," the sheriff said. "This is about the ugliest photo I've ever seen." He threw the driver's license into the pit amongst the logs, and the limbs he'd added from trimming the trees along the dirt trail.

"You got your tape recorder turned on, Sheriff? That's what you're doing, isn't it? You want a confession. I suppose you have my DNA. So, if I confess, are you going to make me a good deal?"

"What makes you think you deserve any deal after what you did?"

"Well, your ass is sitting there alive. That must count for something. I could have killed you and your pansy ass friend and thrown you in the river with a cinder block tied to your damn neck. That's what I should have done."

"Yep, then we wouldn't be here together tonight. Every little decision changes what comes next in our lives," the sheriff said, still twirling the kitchen match.

"Got your tape machine turned on, Sheriff? Here's my confession. I stuck my big, fat dick in your tiny, virgin ass, and it was good." He laughed. His hands were tied together at the wrists. He reached down and unfastened his pants. He wasn't wearing underwear. He pulled himself out.

"Lookie here, I'm getting hard just thinking about your ass. I'm hung like a horse, ain't I? I popped your cherry ass, didn't I? You loved it too, didn't you? Oh, that's right, I forgot to go slow and easy. I guess I did ram it in all at once. That's why you were screaming like a little girl. That's what I did when my daddy did me. I probably stretched you so big, you've been pooping your pants ever since." Carl laughed at the sheriff. "Want a little more, Sheriff?" Carl asked as he rubbed himself with both hands.

Sheriff Raymer stood, pointed his 9mm Glock, and fired, hitting Carl Mitchell's penis. Carl screamed in agony. He moaned and groaned for another ten minutes while the sheriff drank his beer. Then Carl muttered, "You crazy fucker! What the hell? You're so damn jealous of my big dick, you got to shoot it, you damn asshole! I'm going to kill you. I wish I had killed you while I was fucking your asshole and you were doing that little girl scream.

"Speaking of little girls, I popped that cherry for little blonde Emma, didn't I? I heard later, she's seventeen. Damn, I thought she was about thirteen. The young ones really turn me on and make my dick hard as a fucking rock. Hey, I ran into her the other day at a store over in Sulphur Springs. She was buying a pregnancy test. She's late. I had a little chat with her. She's gonna be having my baby before long. How about that? I'm gonna be a daddy. You're supposed to congratulate me. Emma seemed upset about it though. She screamed, but that just turned me on all the more. Too bad I had to leave so fast. I would have had some more fun with her.

"Tell me, Sheriff, you've got a little girl, don't you? What's her name? How old is she? Isn't she about sixteen? I've seen her before. I've watched her. I'll have some of that when I get done with your ass!"

Sheriff Raymer's blood pressure had been steadily rising as he listened to Carl. The thought of Carl with his daughter Julie was the last straw for him. He struck the white tip of the kitchen match on his thumbnail. It sprang to life, and he threw it toward the burn pit. Still in midair, the match found gasoline fumes and ignited the entire pit and its contents. Carl screamed and cursed but was quickly overcome by smoke.

The sheriff took a few steps back and sat in his chair. He raised his beer bottle in a toast. "Don't worry, Emma, he won't bother you anymore."

Sheriff Raymer set his beer on the stump and picked up Carl Mitchell's wallet. He went through each compartment. He set the money aside, gathered everything else, and threw it into the fire. He counted out $2,500 in $100 bills and put it in his pocket.

CHAPTER 22

Like Father, Like Son

Leave me alone. Get out of the way. Let me by," Millie Watson said. Six boys from the senior class, including Ray Raymer, the sheriff's son, stood around her. The boys had been standing together behind the gym as Millie walked from the track field, back to the girl's locker room inside the gym. Millie was in the eleventh grade. As she approached, the group mentioned her looks.

"Would you kiss her, Steve?" Ray Raymer asked, grinning.

"Sure, I would," Steve said.

"What about you, Mike?" Mike and all the others agreed they'd all kiss her.

"I hear she's a little wild and might be prone to do more than kiss," said Ray.

"Would you pop her bra, Steve?"

"You better know it," said Steve. Their game continued, and everyone agreed.

"Would you suck her tits, Mike?" Ray asked.

"In a frickin' heartbeat, I would," Mike said.

She was getting closer to them. They lowered the volume but kept talking.

"Ray, why don't you kiss her, dude?" said Steve. "She's ripe for the picking."

Ray stepped away from the others into the pathway where she walked.

"Hi, Millie, got a second?" She stopped. Ray positioned himself between her and the boys behind him, leaning on the gym wall, so she wouldn't be distracted by them.

"You looked great out there on the track today. I mean you were great out there. The track team is lucky to have you," Ray said. His cheeks turned red.

"Well, today wasn't my best time, and I'm all windblown," she said. She reached up and smoothed her hair.

Ray reached up and moved a few strands to behind her ear, saying, "This one's a little wild too. But you're beautiful."

She smiled and blushed. His hand tarried beside her cheek. "Millie, would you like to go out sometime?" Before she could answer, he added, "Would you mind... would it be all right, if I kiss you?"

She smiled again, flattered by his attention. He moved closer.

"Yes," she said. He kissed her. Behind him, the other five boys burst into laughter. Millie pulled back. He kept one arm around her.

"Don't mind them, Millie. They're just jealous. I'll walk with you." He tried to direct her away from them.

"Hey, what about a kiss for us, Millie?" Steve yelled.

"Was it good, Ray?" Mike asked. "Did you pop her bra?" They walked toward Millie and Ray.

"Cool it, guys. Back off," Ray said. "Come on, Millie, let's

114

go." Ray tried to put some distance between them, but they were already surrounding them.

"Where's my kiss?" Each of the other boys repeated the phrase.

"Stop it, guys." Ray yelled at them.

Mike grabbed Ray's collar on either side with both hands. "You're the one who started this game, Raymer. Get out of the way." Mike slung him around and onto the ground.

"This was a game!" Millie said, staring at Ray on the ground. Their eyes met.

"No, Millie," he said.

The others surrounded her closer. "I'm ready for my kiss, now," Steve said. Millie pushed him away. The others touched her breasts, her butt, her back, her thighs. She whirled from one to the next, removing their hands or pushing them back. Steve moved in, grabbed her, and had his lips on hers. She struggled in his grip.

Ray Raymer grabbed Steve, pulled him back, and decked him with the right cross his father had taught him years ago. "Leave her alone, I said. Are you all right, Millie?"

"Just a game, huh?" Millie said.

"No, Millie," Ray said, but she was already running.

"They did what?" Sheriff Raymer raised his voice when the principal at his son's high school started telling him what had happened. "Stupid idiots," he said.

Principal Fred Stevens told the sheriff the details he had learned from interviewing each boy and Millie Watson, all separately.

"These kids," Sheriff Raymer said. "Don't they know that's sexual assault?"

"The girl doesn't want anyone charged with anything. She said she's happy with them being suspended. The worst of it was Steve's kiss while holding her, both against her will. The other boys touched a bit, all on the exterior of her clothes. It could have been worse if your son hadn't stopped it. Your son kissed her, but they both said he actually asked her permission, and she said yes. His fault was getting the other boys all riled up, hot and bothered, in the first place. It seemed like he was playing the game with them, but then when he went to talk with her, he left all that behind and was really serious about her. Meanwhile, she's not sure if he was playing their game and just jerking her around, or if he was sincere with her. I'm glad I'm not a teenager anymore," said Principal Fred Stevens.

"Me too," said the sheriff. "Fred, I think it would be good if all the boys and their parents met with Millie and her parents on the first day back at school from suspension, for each of those boys to apologize to her. That would clear the air a little and make things less awkward for her when she sees them in the hallways."

"I think that's a good idea. I'll arrange it," said the principal.

"What if we were to do an assembly for the high school kids, and talk with them about sexual assault, rape, and domestic violence. I could do a part on the laws and how a conviction would affect their future. Betty and Jerry from the Rape Crisis Center could talk about things from a victim's viewpoint and about counseling. They've got a lot of brochures they can give out."

"I think that's a great idea. I'll pull in our counselor, and we'll look at our schedule. We should be able to work it out. Maybe we could make it an annual event near the first of each school year if y'all are willing."

"I know I am, and I'm sure Betty and Jerry will be too. They might need some funding help for brochures, but I think it'll work out."

❖❖❖

"What in the Sam Hill were you thinking, son? You didn't, but all of your friends committed a crime today, sexual assault. And you set them up for it. What were you thinking?"

"I guess I wasn't thinking. At first, I just thought it would be fun, but I didn't know one of the guys was gonna say something to me about kissing her. And then when I went to talk to her, I realized how much I really like her. I asked her out."

"That's not the way to have fun, son."

"Well, that's what you and your friends did outside the diner that day. Everybody there seemed to be having fun."

Jack was quiet.

"I guess we modeled that for you. We taught you that. I'm sorry. You know what, son? You and I are a lot more alike than we even knew. You really like this girl, what's her name?"

"Millie."

"You like Millie, and guess what, I like Angelica, the lady that walked past us that day at the diner. And we've both screwed up in the same way, except you got a kiss and I didn't. You're ahead of your dad.

"I want you to know that here a while back, something happened with me that caused me to have an epiphany where women are concerned. I realized I hadn't been treating them with the respect they deserve, that I had sometimes made off-color jokes at their expense and was involved in stuff with the guys like that day in front of the diner and loads more. I'm trying to do better. I really am trying. Some of the things I've done have been habits of mine for a long time, but as I catch myself doing or saying something I shouldn't, I try to change it. Maybe you can change your attitudes and develop good habits concerning women starting now. If you do, I guarantee you'll have a much happier life.

"I think we both need to apologize to these two ladies we like. I talked with your principal about setting up a meeting for you all to apologize to Millie on your first day back to school."

"Dad, I don't want to wait that long. I don't want her to hate me that long. Maybe I could go tomorrow to see her."

"You want me to go with you, son?"

"That would be great. I'm afraid her parents won't let me see her if you aren't with me. Thanks, Dad."

"We'll go tomorrow. Let's get you home. I love you, son. I'll always love you."

CHAPTER 23

Jake's Roof

Hey, Billy. I'm calling to tell you about my visit with Jake Dawsey," said Sheriff Raymer.

"I'm glad you called, Jack. I've been worried about that. What did you find out? Did he look like someone who might blackmail us?"

"No, you don't have to worry about that. He's a good man who wanted to save us from embarrassment." The sheriff told Billy all the details of his visit, except the part about the two bags of evidence he took possession of and later burned.

"Taking him potato salad, pie, and barbecue was a nice touch."

"Speaking of that. Old Jake's house has an old tin-top roof on it, and it's leaking. It's a small house. I was thinking, it wouldn't take very many supplies to replace the roof. His income is low, so he's been catching water in pots and pans. Don't you have a brother-in-law who owns a building supply store?"

"Yes, I do. Old Jake doesn't have a family to replace his roof?"

"His wife died about eight years ago. They only had one son, John Dawsey. You might remember him from school. He was younger than us, and was the kicker on the football team when we were seniors. After college, he moved up north to Michigan. There was a car accident that killed him ten years ago. So, Old Jake is alone. He's seventy-two."

"Well, it wouldn't just be the supplies. Somebody's got to put the roof on the house."

"I was thinking me and you, and about a dozen boys from Ray's senior class, and we could have it done in one Saturday. Do you have a couple of men from your church that would help too? Isn't there a roofer that goes to church with you? Do you know him very well?"

"He put our last roof on at the house we're in now," said Billy.

"Well, all right then. You could ask him to help. He could be our foreman."

"You keep talking like we're really doing this."

"Well, why not? Let's do. There's gotta be a little gratitude somewhere inside of you. Do you realize what he did for us? He dipped up some river water and used paper towels to clean our backsides so well that our butts escaped the notice of the nurses and the doctor in the ER. He dressed us. It's hard to put clothes on an unconscious man, but he did it for both of us before calling 911. He did all that to save us embarrassment and having the whole county know what happened, and in your case, the whole state. Besides all that, it'll make you look like a good guy." Jack laughed.

"Hey, now you're talking. I could bring the press, couldn't I?"

"I figured you'd get around to that. But if it gets a roof on the house, so be it. Old Jake is easy going. He probably won't care, but I have to ask him. If he says no, then no cameras. Agreed?"

"Yeah, yeah, okay. I think my brother-in-law can order the supplies for us and have them delivered right to Jake's house. So, I'm fairly sure we can get it for cost plus shipping. Maybe the roofer can work up the list of supplies we'll need to order. You go be charming and see if anybody else will go in with us to pay for the supplies."

"I'll do it. In fact, I've already gotten one donation of $2,500 to go toward the supplies. I'll talk with Old Jake about it and line up some of the senior class boys to help."

CHAPTER 24

Banished

"Emma, Noah said for me to come out here. What are you doing out here?" Hayden asked. "And where have you been? I haven't seen you at school this week."

"I told Momma I'm pregnant."

"Oh my God, what did she say?"

"Come on in. Have a seat. First, she was mad that I bought a pregnancy test. She thought I bought it here in River Rock and someone might have seen me buying it. After I told her I bought it in Sulphur Springs, she wasn't so mad anymore. Then she didn't say anything for a while, but she soon got over that. After she thought about it a while, she said I could stay out here. The people who owned this property before us rented out this garage apartment. We've just used it for extra storage. Momma got right on it and had Daddy and Noah haul all the old stuff to a donation center for needy families."

"She kicked you out of the house! I can't believe she'd do that to you."

"She did. She's afraid someone will come to the house and see me. I'm not showing yet, but she doesn't want anyone to know I'm pregnant."

"I thought she wanted you to keep the baby and raise it?"

"I don't think she knows exactly what she wants except she would like to pretend I'm not having a baby at all. Since she can't do that, she's hiding me, at least for now."

"Are you quitting school? Tell me you're not quitting."

"I don't want to quit. But she doesn't want me to go."

"Emma, you only lack the rest of this year to finish. How can you not finish?"

"Oh, and guess what? I got the scholarship to the University of Alabama, a full scholarship! Want to see the package?"

"Sure, I do." Emma showed her the letter. They talked about the specifics of going and what's included in the scholarship, as though she would be going.

"Oh, Emma. I'm so sorry it's happening this way. So, you'll stay here until the baby comes?"

"Hayden, you know I don't want this fetus to ever be a baby. I know what I was taught all my life. But I cannot stand the thought of having this thing inside of me, put there by that scum of the earth. I can't stand to think about bringing a son into this world who might turn out to be just like his violent, rapist father. I still want an abortion. Will you drive me to get it if I can find a place to do it?"

"Are you absolutely sure beyond a shadow of a doubt, this is what you want?"

"Yes, I'm positive."

"All right, whatever you need me to do. I'm here for you, girlfriend. I'll do anything you want. I can't believe she has banished you from the house. It's not your fault. You didn't do anything wrong. This is so unfair."

"Oh, that's the other thing. She has started saying things like, 'You shouldn't have been out after dark.' And, 'You always have worn too much makeup.' Oh, and, 'You wear your clothes too tight.' I reminded her I had on sweat pants, a baggy long sleeve T-shirt, and no makeup that night. I had just gotten out of the shower and put that on when she started fussing because Noah wasn't home."

"Why is she trying to make it be your fault you got raped?" Hayden asked. "That makes me so mad with your mom, especially because she knows you didn't do anything wrong."

"I don't know. She's also trying to find one of those Christian schools for wayward girls where everyone is pregnant. She wants to send me there and then let them arrange an adoption. I should tell her if I have it, I'm going to keep it, and let everyone see that her daughter had a child out of wedlock. I wonder how she'd take that news."

"Emma, is there any part of you that wants to keep the baby?" Hayden asked.

"No. There is no fiber of my being that wants to bear a baby by that rapist. And I'm not going to. I've just got to find some help."

"Emma, if you need anything, just let me know."

"There's one thing. She took my phone because she's afraid I might tell the world I'm pregnant. I have some money saved up from my job. Will you take some and get me a new phone? I need to be looking for some help with my problem and want to be able to call you. It needs to be a smart phone, so I have internet, but one of those pay-as-you-go. I can use the Wi-Fi here. Probably nobody will notice."

"Sure. You know I'll do anything for you. I'll bring it tomorrow."

"When you come back, stash it in your pocket and come straight out here instead of going to the house." Emma gave her money for the phone.

"Okay, I will."

"There's one more thing, Hayden. When you come to the door here, say who you are after you knock. I'm afraid to open the door because it might be one of the rapists."

"Oh, Emma, surely not. How would any of them know where to find you? Even if they do, why would they come here?"

Emma reminded her about what Carl did and said outside the store in Sulphur Springs. "They have my address because they have my driver's license and now, he thinks I'm pregnant. He talked about us having a baby together. I'm scared he might come back."

"Oh no! You can always come and stay with me at my house. My folks won't care."

"My mother would. It wouldn't work with her plan to hide me from the world."

"Emma, anytime. You just call, and I'll come and get you, wherever you are. All right, I'll bring the phone tomorrow."

"Thank you, Hayden. I knew you'd help me." They hugged goodbye.

CHAPTER 25

Amends

"Sarah, I want to apologize to you." Sheriff Raymer sat at the kitchen table in the house where they had lived together before the divorce. He had thought they would be there together for the rest of their lives. They were high school sweethearts. He was the handsome quarterback on the football team. Sarah was smart and beautiful. She had helped him with algebra so he could stay on the team. She had agreed to wait for him when he had joined the Marines after high school. She had started classes at the community college wearing his engagement ring. When he had finished basic training and had come home on leave, they had married.

"For what?" she asked. She handed him creamer and sugar for his coffee.

Jack cleared his throat. He didn't know how to start. He couldn't remember ever saying he was sorry to Sarah, for anything. He looked down at the table. "For all the times I didn't listen to you," he said. He looked up into her eyes and quickly back to the tablecloth.

"What are you talking about?" Sarah asked. She sat beside him. "Jack, what's going on? Are you, all right? You look like you've healed. Has something happened?"

"I'm sorry," he managed. "I'm sorry for all the times I yelled at you, for the times I ignored you, and the times I couldn't see you because I was lost in my own misery." He slowly raised his gaze to her face and looked into her eyes. She stared at him. "I've had a lot of time to think about it. I want you to know I'm a different man now than I was when we were together. And I'm sorry for how I was with you. Can you forgive me?"

"Are you trying to get me to take you back? Because if you are.... Look, Jack, I might manage to forgive you, but don't you think for one minute that asking for forgiveness is going to make me want to take you back. Just because you want forgiveness doesn't mean you won't go right back to doing the exact same things all over again. I don't trust you in that area. It took me a long time to get to where I am now, and I'm not about to take you back, just like that!"

"I understand. That'll be all right. I will be grateful if you can find it in your heart to forgive me."

"All right, Jack. I think I can. I'll give it a try. Where is all this coming from?"

"I just want you to know that I've changed. I realize now what I've done wrong with you in the past, and I know you deserved better and still do. I'll always have feelings for you. I will always want the best for you and our kids. Sarah, is there anything you need? Let me make it up to you by helping, if there's anything you need."

"I'll tell you what I need. I need you to spend some time with your daughter. She's seeing a boy who treats her just like you treated me. She has picked out someone just like she remembers her dear old dad. She thinks she's in love.

She's a smart girl, but she's imitating what she saw all those years, and she should have better."

"I'll do it, Sarah. I'll show her how a young man should treat her."

"Thank you, Jack. If you can get through to her, I will be eternally grateful. She won't listen to anything I tell her."

"I'll take her on a dinner date Saturday night. Let me know if that time works, okay?"

CHAPTER 26

Bright Ideas

I hate meeting here, but I know we're a lot less likely to be seen together here than anywhere else," Sheriff Raymer said. Senator Billy had contacted him for a meeting and the sheriff told Billy to meet him at the crime scene. "This really is a beautiful place back in here beside the river and so shady with the huge old trees. I'd love it if I could keep those memories out of my head." The sheriff climbed into the passenger side of Billy's truck.

"Is all this cloak and dagger and not being seen together stuff really necessary, Jack? You may be paranoid. After all, we live in the same city, we're both public servants, and we've known one another for ages. Why wouldn't it be normal for us to sometimes run into each other and have a chat?"

"Yes, I think it's the thing to do. So, what's going on with you?"

"I wanted to tell you I'm writing some legislation which, if passed, will require the state to fund the state crime labs better, and require funding for all the rape kits to be processed, the backlog, and all going forward. It will require tracking of the rape kits and will allow victims to know the status of their kits. There's also some language in there which will help different groups of law enforcement to work better together, more seamlessly, to catch and prosecute sexual predators. I've done a lot of research on all of this and frankly, Jack, I'm just blown away that all of this has been allowed to continue for such a long time. It's inconceivable to me. It's like you told me; there are a lot of serial rapists out there, who, if convicted, would be off the streets and not continuing to rape. Allowing them to continue is a travesty of justice."

"Wow, look at you. You're doing something to help the people and actually earning your title of 'the candidate who is tough on crime.' I'm proud of you, Billy, soon to be Governor Billy," said the sheriff.

"Jack, you should run for my Senate seat after I move over to the governor's mansion. Aside from this little secret of ours out here, you don't have any other skeletons in your closet, do you?"

"Are you kidding me? No, Billy. It'll never happen. Skeletons, wow, define that. Man, I was a Marine for twenty years. I served in Kosovo, Bosnia, Afghanistan, and Iraq. The American people sent me and thousands of others there to protect and serve, which, in this case, means to kill people.

"I was a good soldier, and I killed people I didn't even know, that I had no personal beef with, and who were probably a lot like me and were there doing the same thing. But you know, if any of us had come home and killed some thug who had raped his twelve-year-old daughter, we'd be sitting on death row waiting for the electric chair because we're no longer at war. No, Billy, I don't need to be a senator."

"Jack, you're a genius! I knew if I spent time with you, I would get what I need for my campaign. I'll start it now and continue it when I run for governor."

"What are you talking about?"

"I'll ask Alabamians to declare war on sexual assault in all of its nasty forms. And I hope the nation will do the same. Thank you, Jack. I've got it all flooding into my mind. That's what needs to happen. When I first thought about that 'tough on crime' platform, I confess, I never knew I would really mean it. But with what happened to us, I do, and I can work toward making changes to help a lot of people. I'm going to use your words, Jack. Don't worry, I won't mention your name."

"Look, Billy, with you running for governor, and until all this blows over and is buried, you can see why we don't need to be seen together. If anything ever comes up about me in the eyes of the public, you'll be happy to be able to say we're not close, and to deny all knowledge of anything that will disparage you. That's what you do, Billy. Promise me, if anyone ever suspects anything about things I may or may not have done, you deny knowledge and distance your-self from me. And you're already not telling anything about what happened here that day. Got it, Billy? Promise?"

"Thank you, Jack. I still promise all of that. You're always taking care of others. I hope you'll do something good for yourself sometime. Speaking of which, did you ever go out with that pretty lady who walked past us that day? The one who wouldn't speak to you?"

"No, but maybe I need to follow up with her," the sheriff said. "I owe her an apology. I'll see you around, Billy. I really am proud of what you're doing."

"Thank you, Jack. Be careful out there. I worry about you."

CHAPTER 27

R-E-S-P-E-C-T

Look, Mom. Daddy brought me roses!" Julie said. "Did he ever bring you roses?"

"Yes, he did. All the time. And he sent some of them even when he was out of the country." Sarah lied like a dishonest used car salesman, and then winked at Jack when their daughter wasn't looking. The sheriff winced with regret and knew why she had lied. They were on a mission together to retrain their daughter on what she should expect from a man who wants her attention. It was a tactical lie utilized for a greater purpose. Still, Jack was impressed with Sarah's skill and ease with the lie.

"Would you like to take them with you, honey, or put them in water and leave them on the dresser in your room for later?" Jack asked.

"I don't want them to get messed up, so I'll put them in my room," Julie said and left to find a vase.

"My, but you look nice," Sarah said. "You got a haircut,

didn't you? Jack, I am impressed. Thank you for doing this. I hope it works."

"Me too. But I'm happy to spend time with my daughter and should have been doing it all along." Then he whispered, "I'm impressed. You're a great liar." He laughed.

Julie rejoined them. "Ready to go, princess?" Jack held his hand out to her. She took his left hand, and he reached for the door with his right.

"You look very pretty tonight, Julie," Jack said. He knew she had dressed up more than usual. She wore a lovely pink dress and had put up her hair.

"Thank you, Daddy." She smiled.

They reached the car. He opened the door for her and continued holding her hand as she got into the car and then closed the door. Soft music played in the car.

"Where are we going, Daddy?"

"I want to take you to supper, if that's all right with you. Have you eaten?"

"No, I haven't."

"Have you ever been to the Cyprus Inn on Lake Ann?"

"No, but I remember one of my friends went there and said it was great."

"Would you like to go there?"

"Yes, I'd love to," Julie said, glowing.

The hostess at the restaurant showed them to a table in front of a large plate-glass window, overlooking the beautiful waters of Lake Ann. The sun was getting low in the sky and would soon be sliding into the water on the horizon. Blue, gold, and orange horizontal streaks already framed the sun as it sank lower and lower in the sky.

"This is a great table. What a view. Daddy, what made you want to bring me out tonight?"

"Well, it looks like we're jumping right into the thick of

things." He paused. She waited. "Julie, I haven't been in your life enough since your mother and I divorced. When I was there before the divorce, I didn't set a good example of how a man should treat and speak to his wife. I regret that."

"What do you mean?"

"I want you to know that the way I behaved back then isn't the way a man should treat a woman, any woman, but especially one he loves. If it's not too late, I want to try to correct things with you. I want you to know I've changed, and I want you to be treated much better than what you witnessed back then, by everyone, but especially anyone who wants to spend time around you. In fact, I want you to insist that everyone treat you well, with dignity and respect. If there's anyone who doesn't treat you that way, they don't deserve your friendship, and especially not your love. That's what I've had on my mind, in a nutshell. There's more, but that's enough for now. We have to order, and we have a sunset to watch."

"Daddy, is this about a boy or something? Cause you can't tell me who to date."

"I'm not telling you who to date," he said slowly and quietly. "I'm asking you to pick someone who values you as a person, who respects you, and treats you well, all the time."

"Did Momma say something to you about Zack?"

"No, your mother hasn't mentioned anyone named Zack to me. Is that one of your friends?"

"I'm not so sure."

"Sweetheart, this is about anybody, male or female. Surround yourself with people who treat you well, with respect, and don't let anyone take up your time if they don't treat and speak to you with respect. Sometimes it might be a good idea, when someone says or does something to you, to ask yourself, 'would someone who values and respects me do or say that?' And remind yourself that you deserve respect."

"What are you getting to eat, Daddy?"

"Well, I was looking at the grilled fish, but I think instead, I'm getting the fried fish, with a green salad and baked potato. They have marvelous onion rings here. How about if I order those to eat along with what would have been our healthy salad?"

"That sounds great. I'll do that too, or maybe the shrimp."

"They also serve bread pudding a la mode here. Something to think about."

Over salad and onion rings, they watched a flock of geese returning to the safety of the pond for their overnight roosting. Jack touched his daughter's hand to draw her attention, pointing to their silhouettes against the setting sun. She held his hand for a moment.

"I thought geese slept in trees overnight. Why are they coming back to the water?"

"Geese are a little heavy to roost in trees. On the ground, they are very vulnerable to attack by their enemy, I mean predators. Sleeping on the water, their predators can't quickly sneak up on them. They even trade off guard duty all through the night."

"How do you know stuff like that?"

"Every once in a while, your old Dad learns something new." He laughed. "There's even a saying, 'Even a blind squirrel finds a nut every once in a while.' I wonder if that was written about me." Julie laughed with him.

"Thank you, Daddy. This is nice. You make me feel special."

"You are special, sweetheart. Don't ever forget that. Don't make excuses for people who don't treat you that way."

"Daddy, why didn't you treat Mom better?"

135

"Hmm, that's a big question. I've got in mind a trip I'd like us to take together if you're interested. Maybe we can talk about that question on the trip."

"What trip?"

"Would you like to go to tour the Space Center in Huntsville, Alabama? Are you still as interested in space as you were when you were younger?"

"Oh, Daddy, that would be wonderful. I've always wanted to go there."

"Okay then, get me the dates of your next break from school, and I'll make reservations. On the way there and back, you can ask me anything. Make a list if you want to."

"Anything? Really?"

"Yes, anything. If you can stand to ask it and hear the answer, then I can stand to talk about it. Even the tough stuff."

"So, if I ask you about sex, you're going to answer my question?"

"Yep, I am. We should be able to talk about anything. I don't imagine you'll ask about something unless you want to know the answer or are at least curious."

They finished their meal, and he took her home, opening doors for her and holding her hand. He listened to everything she said. Back on Julie's porch, he thanked her for the evening, they hugged, and he kissed her on the forehead.

"I love you, Daddy."

"I love you too, sweetheart, always and forever."

CHAPTER 28

Starting Over

Angelica, please. Please wait. Would you slow down?" The sheriff had such good results with his ex-wife and daughter that he found courage enough to try to apologize to Angelica, but so far, she was having none of it.

"I don't want to talk to you! You know I'm on my way to work, and I can't be late. You know how Judge Williams is." Angelica Lopez was a stenographer and was headed to the courthouse on the square. Sheriff Raymer watched for her every morning. Up until the laughing incident outside the diner, they had both exchanged morning greetings and warm smiles.

"This'll only take a minute. Angelica, please." He put his hand under her arm. She turned suddenly, recoiling from his touch. He threw both hands up, palms outward.

"Would you sit for just a minute and then I'll leave you alone?" he said and motioned to the bench behind her. She sat, folding her arms across her chest.

"Well," she said. "What do you want? You have one minute."

"I want you to forgive me," Sheriff Raymer said.

"It doesn't matter if I forgive you, because I don't want anything to do with you."

"Angelica," he started and then went down on one knee in front of her. "I am sorry for my behavior and the behavior of the goons I stood with in front of the diner on the day we all laughed. It was atrocious, and I've had time to think about it. If men had treated my daughter or a wife of mine that way, I would be fighting mad. Please forgive me and give me another chance to be in your life. Let me take you out sometime to make it up to you."

"Get up. People are staring at us," she said. He sat on the bench next to her.

"You want to make it up to me and be in my life. Okay, you pick me up for church this Sunday. We'll go to church and then you can take me out to lunch. We'll see how much you really want to be in my life. I have to go to work now."

Sunday came and Sheriff Raymer arrived on time at Angelica's townhouse door. She opened the door, and he presented her with a bouquet of pink roses, catching her off guard.

"Oh my, they're very pretty," she said. "Come in, I'll put them in water." He followed her to the kitchen and laid a box of chocolates on the counter.

"You shouldn't have," she said.

"I have a lot of making up to do," he said. "This is a nice place you have here. How long have you lived here?"

"Fifteen years, ever since my husband passed away," she said. "After he died, I sold the house we had. It was in a rural area. It was big and seemed to always need some repair or maintenance of some kind or another. He had always taken care of that stuff and cutting the grass and trimming the bushes. The place was too much for me to handle on my own. So, I moved here. It's close to work which is also nice."

"I'm sorry for your loss," Jack said. "I thought you might be divorced. Are we going to the Catholic church this morning?"

"I sometimes go there with family when they are visiting, but most of the time, I go to the Greatest Love Baptist Church. It's closer, and it gets the job done for me." She laughed. "I know my Catholic family would probably choke me for saying that, but I don't think God cares too much about which church we go to." Her laugh was warm and inviting. Her smile came easily. He could feel a shift in her. She was no longer defensive and trying to push him away. He reached out for her hand.

"May I?" he asked. She let him take it. He pulled her closer.

"You've forgiven me, haven't you? I can feel it," he said. He stared into her eyes, and she didn't look away. He kissed her gently.

"Yes," she mumbled, "I thought it best."

"That makes me happy," he said and hugged her tightly. "We better go if we want to be on time," he said.

❖❖❖

They arrived at the church. "Hello, Sheriff, Angelica," said the deacon greeting everyone at the front door. He shook Sheriff Raymer's hand. "Glad you could make it today." He gave them a church bulletin.

"I haven't been to church in a good while," Jack whispered to Angelica.

"Don't worry, it probably hasn't changed very much," she said.

"Where do you usually sit?"

"About half way up on the right. I'll show you." She took his hand.

"Everyone is looking at me," he said.

She knew it was true and thought it funny that such a big man was nervous about attending church. "No, they're looking at me," she said. "They always look at me because I'm beautiful." She giggled, and he smiled. "It'll be all right. Don't worry, Jack."

He was glad to be seated on the cushioned pew. He put his arm on the back of the pew and around Angelica. She looked up at him and grinned. He remembered he'd always liked the music better than the sermons. He still felt that way but was surprised to find he liked what the pastor had to say. His emotions had run the gamut since his rape. He found himself touched by the pastor's words and wished he'd not been listening. The pastor quoted a verse from the Bible, "Come to me, all of you who are weary and burdened, and I will give you rest." The pastor said a prayer at the end of his sermon. The sheriff felt a stirring inside.

The music director announced the closing hymn, *Precious Lord Take My Hand*, and everyone sang as the pastor announced the altar call. He invited anyone who felt led, to come to pray or receive prayer. The church had padded cushions at the front of the church in front of the raised platform. This was designed to allow people to kneel on the cushions, rest their arms on the raised platform, and pray, or to be counseled by the pastor, or prayed for there. The stirring in the sheriff's soul continued. He excused himself and knelt at the altar to pray. The surprised pastor joined him and prayed for him.

❖❖❖

"Jack, are you all right?" Angelica asked him.

"I'm fine. I guess I needed to pray," he said. "It's been a long time." He was clearly fighting his emotions.

"We don't have to go to lunch if you feel like you need to go home," Angelica offered.

"Are you kidding? A pretty lady said she has forgiven me, and she'd let me take her to lunch. You don't think I'm giving that up, do you? I've been thinking about spending time with you for a long time. It's been a fantasy for me, that you might actually like me. I don't know why I waited so long to ask you out. And, I don't know why I said that. Men don't usually spill the beans like that. I want to be straight with you, Angelica. I've been in the Marines and have been a sheriff, and through the years I've done a lot of bad things. I guess I have a lot of things I need to pray about. Did I embarrass you?"

"Oh, no. Of course not. That's what people do in church. It's good that you connected with your spiritual side and with God."

They went to lunch, talking and laughing easily. Back at the door to her home, the sheriff asked, "Would you like to join me next Saturday for a paddle boat cruise up the Muscogee River?"

"I'd love to. That sounds like a wonderful outing. I didn't know there was such a thing."

They swapped phone numbers and shared a hug and another kiss before he said goodbye.

CHAPTER 29

Noah's Forensics

How's it going, Noah? Are you making much progress on your special assignment?" Sheriff Raymer asked Noah. The sheriff had the names and addresses of all the men involved in Emma's rape, but he wanted to help Noah stay busy.

"Hi, Sheriff. Yes, sir. I'll show you. I've created a spreadsheet for the data. I did a separate page for each name, just like you said. They are all in the same spreadsheet file with different pages. I have a summary page up front, summarizing the data from each page. Here on the Oliver page, you can see all the different last names, with other fields for age, address, city, state, telephone number. Of course, I don't have all the data for all of them, but where available, I have it listed here."

"This looks good, Noah. Where did you get your data?"

"Here's the field, at the end. See in the last column. I've listed the sources."

"Are those photos I see?"

"Yes, sir. I was able to get some. I accessed some high school yearbooks that were posted online. For those, I got the photos and then searched social media sites, as well, for other information. For the ones from yearbooks, I assumed an approximate age based on their grade, the date of the yearbook, and assuming they passed each grade. You can see here, in some of the fields, I have listed clickable links where you can go directly to the source."

"Noah, this is impressive. I like the way your mind works. I signed you up for a monthly digital forensics magazine. It has current information and future trends in forensics. I thought you might be interested. I didn't want to give them your home address or any of your personal information, so I wrote you up as Noah Volunteer and used the address here and the email we established for you. Here's the site and the information for it." The sheriff handed him a printed sheet of information.

"Wow, that sounds interesting," Noah said.

"There are a lot of good jobs in forensics, if you're interested," the sheriff said, grinning.

"I will email you the hyperlink to this spreadsheet, Sheriff. Then you can see it anytime. I'm still adding to it. I haven't exhausted all of my ideas yet for data sources."

"I'm impressed, Noah. Great job. How about I take you to lunch to say thank you, and you can tell me how your sister's doing while we're there?"

They went to Lorenzo's Pizza Italiano, which Noah said was the best in town. The sheriff agreed with him.

"So, how's your sister doing? Everything going all right for her at school?"

"Momma made her quit school," Noah said, shaking his head.

"What? There's not many months left in the school year, is there?"

"Momma said Emma would be showing soon, and she doesn't want anybody to know Emma's pregnant. Plus, there's the gym class thing, and Momma doesn't trust her not to tell anybody."

"Maybe there might be a way she could study at home and take her tests there and still be able to finish on time."

"That would be great. I'll mention it to Emma and Momma tonight. Momma made Emma move to the garage apartment, so no one would see her if they come to the house. We had things stored there, but we cleaned it out and Emma moved in."

"Noah, I don't mean to butt into family business, but Emma doesn't need to be isolated from her family right now. She needs to know and feel like she's supported."

"I think so too, Sheriff. Momma and Daddy both act like they can't stand to be around her now. I hang out with her some, but sometimes she won't let me. I worry about her. Did she tell you... she doesn't want to have the baby?"

"She told me. I'm sorry that all of this happened to her, Noah. If I could wave a magic wand and undo it all, I certainly would."

"I would too, Sheriff. I wish we could."

❖❖❖

Back in his office, Sheriff Raymer sat staring at the wall, thinking about Emma. Everything he thought seemed to come out wrong. He tried to imagine a happy ending for her but, try as he might, he couldn't figure it out. He threw his empty plastic water bottle across the length of his office into the opposite corner wall. It hit and fell below into a garbage can he'd put there for moments like this. He left his office early. On the way home, the sheriff stopped for gas. He filled up his truck and two gas cans, one for his riding lawn mower, and one for his other gasoline needs.

CHAPTER 30

Oliver

Sheriff Jack Raymer sat in his truck in a dark corner of the parking lot behind the Hide-a-Way Night Club. It was just over the state line on the Georgia side of the river. He had followed Oliver Banner to the club from his house. He saw Oliver pull in behind the club, and he drove on by. Sheriff Raymer turned around, came back, and parked in front where he noticed lots of Alabama car tags in the parking lot.

Sheriff Raymer went inside the club. He had put on a light weight black jacket and a black knit toboggan. He pulled the 'boggin,' as most called it, down low over his eyebrows, his ears, and hair. He hung back in a dark corner and watched. He saw Oliver come inside from the back door, go to the bar, get a drink, and talk to the bartender. Before leaving, Oliver took an envelope from his breast pocket and slid it across the bar to the bartender. Oliver went out the back door. The bartender reached over to the wall behind the bar and flipped a light switch. A little red light lit up at the top of the wall, to the right of the large wall mirror. Then the sheriff noticed people go, one by one, out the back door, stay a few minutes and come back.

Sheriff Raymer went back to his truck out front and pulled it around back, with his lights off. He eased to the far-right side of the large parking lot behind the club where there were no lights. He watched with binoculars, drug sale after drug sale. Oliver was like an adult, perverted version of the Pinkie Dinkie man selling ice cream from his truck on the street. Sheriff Raymer didn't see anything that looked like cameras and was sure Oliver wouldn't be selling drugs there if cameras were recording.

The sheriff flipped the buttons on his interior lights, so they wouldn't come on when the door opened, and he carefully exited his truck. He stayed in the dark shadows as he moved closer and closer. Dressed in black, he blended in well. He noticed there were three to five minutes between each drug buy transaction.

He was close enough now. When the back door of the club closed after the last buyer, the sheriff stepped out into the light, 9mm Glock drawn.

"What the fuck, man? You don't wanna mess with me," Oliver said, not knowing who he was seeing. The sheriff flashed his badge.

"Hands on your head, and turn around, Oliver."

"Oh my God, it's you! Hey, I haven't been able to find Carl and Dougie lately. Did you have anything to do with that? Did you arrest them?"

"I might have. Hands on your head now and turn around facing your van."

"I didn't see in the River Rock paper where it said anything about them being arrested," Oliver said as he slowly turned, hands on his head.

"You read? You're kidding, right?" The sheriff shoved the Glock in his shoulder holster and moved in to handcuff him. The drug dealer spun around and threw a right cross at the sheriff's face. Jack rocked back, dodging the punch, but caught Oliver's left glancing jab to his forehead. Without a thought, Jack dropped to a low crouch, shoved the thug's arms upward, and rammed his shoulder into Oliver's abdomen. Jack wrapped his hands behind his opponent's knees, chopping down with his right and picking up with his left, taking him to the ground in a double-leg takedown. Jack landed with his shoulder pressing into the waist of his adversary and his right forearm across his neck. Oliver's left hand moved toward his belt, but Jack saw it, stuck his right hand into Oliver's pants, and pulled out a revolver. He tossed it aside, rolled Oliver over, knelt on the small of his back, and slapped the cuffs on him.

Damn, I'm good. I still got it. All that Marine Corps training paid off. I did all that in a flash, without even thinking about what to do.

He left Oliver lying there and turned to the back door of the club. Earlier, the sheriff had spotted, with his binoculars, an old metal pipe leaning against the wall in a corner near the door. He grabbed it and stuck it through the door handle and another metal piece to jam the door so it wouldn't open.

The sheriff opened Oliver's van door with his gloved hand and threw in Oliver's pistol. He saw a paper bag and looked inside. Cash. He stuck it in his jacket pocket. He got Oliver up off the ground, put some tape over his mouth, and walked him out to where the sheriff's truck was parked. He put Oliver in the bed of the truck, tied his feet, and then his feet to the handcuffs. Sheriff Raymer put the tarp over him and drove onto the river bridge going to Alabama.

The sheriff thought as he drove. *Someone will take Oliver's place back at the club. We need to do a road block on this road one night, with the drug dogs, as all these Alabama people head home.*

"This guy's never going to bother Emma again, and he's never going to rape Julie or anyone else's daughter," Sheriff Raymer said aloud into the darkness of his truck cab.

CHAPTER 31

The Meeting

The Kawasaki Ninja H2R roared from full speed to a crawl on Riverside Road as Paul readied to turn into the trail road. He was going to the scene of the crime, the clearing by the Muscogee River where he and the other River Rats had partied and raped Emma, the sheriff, and Senator Billy. Vince was already there.

"How's it going? Man, that's a sweet ride. Where'd you get it?" Vince asked.

"I bought it new, just last week," Paul said as he leaned back onto the seat.

"Damn. Where'd you get the dough for it? Those are frickin' expensive. Over fifty thousand, aren't they?" Vince asked.

"What can I say? Business has been good. Have you seen Dougie around? I've been trying to get up with him. We were supposed to do some business together, but he was a no show," Paul said.

"No, I haven't seen him. I haven't heard from Carl or Oliver lately either. Have you? It's weird," Vince said.

"Come to think of it, I haven't heard from them either, but I hear somebody coming. Maybe it's them," Paul said.

Ned and Bert drove into the clearing together on their motorcycles. They took off their helmets. The sun shone down on the clearing. Ned put on dark sunglasses.

"I thought I'd be the last one here," Ned said. "Where are the others? Have y'all heard from 'em? Carl is most always early or at least on time." He moved over to the picnic table with the others.

"We haven't heard from them," Paul said. "We thought y'all might have."

"When is the last time any of you heard from any of them?" Bert asked.

"It's been awhile, but Dougie and I were supposed to do some business together, and I haven't been able to get a hold of him. I think it's weird. And y'all know we hear from Carl at least once a week. Something's wrong," Paul said.

"Well, let's have a frickin' drink and talk about it," Vince said, laughing.

They opened a bottle of Jack Daniel's and passed it around. Vince unloaded the ice chest from his motorcycle and tossed each of them a beer. The whiskey bottle was soon empty, and Bert pulled out a plastic bag.

"Hey, y'all want some weed? My treat," Bert said. He passed around the bag of already rolled marijuana cigarettes. Everybody lit up. Ned retold one of their favorite exploit stories. They laughed until they cried. They all chimed in with other stories. Paul laughed so hard, he fell off the end of the bench at the picnic table, which made them laugh all the more. As their chuckles subsided, things turned serious.

"Y'all know there's something wrong when Carl, Dougie,

and Oliver all three are not here," said Paul. "It ain't right. None of them have called, and we've tried to call them. And we haven't been able to find them either. Something's happened to them."

"It does seem that way," Bert said.

"Damn straight," said Paul.

"Well, I hate to mention it, but you know that damn sheriff said he was going to kill us all," Ned said. "We should have killed both those guys instead of just leaving them. That was sloppy. We should have dumped them right over there in the Muscogee." He pointed to the fast-moving water a few dozen yards away.

"You really think he might have killed them?" Vince asked. "Damn. If he killed them, that means he'll be coming for the rest of us."

"Carl damn well put him in his place. I don't think he could take Carl," Bert said. "Maybe they were all together and got arrested somewhere or had a car wreck."

"You mean Carl put him in his place after the sheriff got hit in the head and knocked out with a whiskey bottle," Paul said. "Before that, you remember, the sheriff laid Carl out on the ground."

"Yeah, I guess that's right," Bert said.

"Fuck, that means he's doing what he said he would do. He's coming after us. What are we going to do? He's coming after us!" Vince said, looking past his friends to the edge of the woods all around them. He could be behind any of those trees, right now. He could step out and start shooting." The others looked all around.

"Well, if we don't do something, we're just sitting ducks waiting for him to pick us off one by one," Ned said.

"I'm not waiting around for him. I think we should get the hell out of Dodge," Bert said. "Why sit around waiting for him to kill us? We wouldn't know when or where he might show up and take us out."

"Wait a minute, guys. We've got a great business going here," Paul said. "I'm making more than I've ever made in my life. We've got our contacts working and loads of customers. We can't just walk away. There's got to be something else we can do."

"What if we kill him first?" Ned asked.

"Yep, that's what we need to do," Paul said. "Let's do it. I'm in. What about y'all?"

"I'm in," Vince said.

"Me too," said Bert. "It'll be a lot safer for us if we all go together to get him. I've got an AK-47 at the house with his name on it."

"Do any of you know where the sheriff lives?" Ned asked. None did.

"Can any of you get a common-looking car, to use to follow the sheriff? We got to know where to find him," Ned said.

"I can borrow my Momma's car or maybe my sister's," Vince said.

"Great," said Ned. "You go tomorrow and follow him home without being seen. Drive past the place a few times and see how the house and the yard is laid out. Draw it on a piece of paper so we can make our plan." Call me, and then we'll all get together and plan the rest.

"I'll do it," Vince said.

❖❖❖

"Is this Sheriff Raymer?" Old Jake asked. He'd called the cell phone number Jack had written on the back of his business card and given to Old Jake.

"Yes, this is the sheriff."

"This be Old Jake, sir. I thought you might want to know.

Those motorcycle fellas were out here, up the road a piece, again. I had gone to town, so I don't know when they came, but they just left."

"Do you think it was the same ones, Jake?" the sheriff asked.

"Yes, sir, it was, but there wasn't as many of them. I heard them when they cranked up. I walked onto the front porch. I watched them, and only four came out."

"Thank you, Jake. I appreciate you letting me know. I hope you're doing well."

"Yes, sir. I'm fine. Thank you kindly."

CHAPTER 32

"Will You Walk into My Parlor?"

"Said the Spider to the Fly"
(Mary Howitt ~ 1828)

The sheriff was glad to be home. It had been a trying day for him. He got himself a longneck bottle of beer and sat in his favorite chair with Max by his side. He wanted to finish his beer and relax awhile before doing anything else. He took a deep breath and exhaled slowly. Max licked his hand, and the sheriff rubbed his friend behind his ears, just as Max had intended.

"It's great to be home, Maxie. It's the best time of the day," the sheriff said. He was beginning to relax. As his muscles released the vice grip they'd had on the back of his neck, his shoulders, and lower back, he realized just how tense he'd been.

Max's ears perked straight up. He growled low like a bass singer with a bad cold.

The sheriff sat up straight. "Whatcha hear, Maxie?" As he stood, the driveway alarm dinged. He knew someone had walked or driven by the sensor into the driveway. Then the alarm dinged for the back of the property. The sheriff picked up his binoculars and headed to the front of the house. He looked out onto his large front lawn. A shiny black king-cab pickup truck was parked just inside the gate in the driveway, blocking the entrance, which had been open. He followed the perimeter of the lawn with his binoculars.

There you are, you bastards. Two men scurried along the side edge of the property toward the house. He recognized them as two of the rapists. One carried an AK-47, the other a pistol.

The sheriff hurried to the back window, looking out with the binoculars. "There they are, Max." Max growled. "Yes, Max. Good boy."

"I remodeled the house and here they come with pistols and an AK-47, damn it. I don't want them shooting holes in my walls. I don't want them busting in my doors either. Fuck it, I'll just let 'em in. They're coming in anyway," he said aloud. He reached out and opened the back door. He went to the front of the house and opened wide the front door.

"Maxie, come," the sheriff said. He headed to his bedroom. He didn't want Max to get hurt. "Max, let me handle this. It's my problem. I'll take care of it." In his bedroom, he went to the closet, moved his combat medical kit, and flipped the switch to release the secret door. He opened the door and went back into the bedroom. He heard steps on the back deck. Max growled.

"Max, shh," the sheriff said, with his finger to his lips. The sheriff went to the corner of the room to the right of his bed and on the far side of the dresser. "Max, come." Max went to him. "Here, Max, sit." Max went into the corner, faced outward toward the room, and sat down. "Good boy, Max. Stay, Max." The sheriff gave the hand signal he had taught Max for stay. "Good boy, Max."

The sheriff heard the men coming in the front door and

talking with the two who had entered the back door. Max growled. "Max, shh," said the sheriff, again putting his finger to his lips. "Stay, Max." The sheriff went through the closet, got his 9mm Glock and extra ammunition, and moved to the right of the door opening to wait. His pulse rate increased. Then his brain morphed into that of a killer soldier, and everything else fell away as though he'd become a different person. His pulse rate lowered, a calmness spread across his entire being, a certain numbness emerged as he detached, and only his mission remained.

"Look, here's his beer. It's half full and still cold. He's here somewhere. The front door was closed when we drove up. Now it's open. Y'all split up, spread out, and let's find him. Let's get this done and get out of here," said Ned. They each went in different directions.

Ned went in the direction of the sheriff's bedroom. Adrenaline coursed through his veins, his muscles tensed, his breathing was fast and shallow. Ned took tiny steps, hoping not to be heard, but the old wooden planks betrayed him, creaking with each step. The pistol he held shook in spite of its weight, which should have helped to steady his hand.

Ned eased into the bedroom, looking to and fro. He saw the open closet and turned toward it. Max's ears perked up, but he sat still, watching. Ned stepped into the closet and saw the light from the basement shining through the opening going to the landing at the top of the basement stairs.

The sheriff heard the creaking of the floor getting closer. He knew exactly where Ned was. His Glock was secured. He hoped not to need it. He didn't want to use it, as it would draw the attention of the other three thugs. The sheriff watched. A pistol slowly emerged from behind the wall.

"Wow!" Ned whispered, seeing the huge basement and the things in it. "He slipped out a different way." The hand and arm holding the gun continued its progression through the entrance to the basement stairway landing.

The sheriff waited behind the wall. The seconds crawled by. Then he grabbed Ned's wrist with one hand, and the other hand landed behind the elbow. The sheriff twisted, and the gun dropped. Ned followed his arm. The sheriff readjusted his hands and sharply jerked Ned's head, snapping his neck in one smooth motion. The sheriff dragged Ned's body to the far right side of the landing, secured the pistol, and moved back to his waiting position in preparation for the next target.

Paul had searched the kitchen pantry and closets in each of the rooms he entered. He looked under the beds in the guest rooms. All were searching, moving in a counter-clockwise direction. Paul reached the end of his search area and moved into Ned's area. He came to the sheriff's bedroom. He remembered the way the sheriff had easily thrown Carl to the ground back in the woods. At twenty-two years old, Paul was the youngest of the group. He was small built and trim, looking more like a teenager than a man. The gun in his hand made him feel more like a man, but he was nervous. For all his big talk, he had never killed anyone and the only fights he'd ever been in, he had lost. Earning big money selling drugs made him feel important. He loved having so much money to spend after having been poor all his life. He would kill the sheriff rather than go back to being poor.

"I can do this. Let's do it and get out of here," Paul whispered. He saw the sheriff's open closet and looked inside. He saw the open door going out the other side. Bright light shone into the closet from the basement. "Well I'll be, would you look at that. What the fuck is that?" He said softly as he eased slowly toward it, step by step.

Max obediently sat still, watching, waiting.

Paul's gun emerged from the closet into the opening of the basement. "He's got a secret escape route like those pirates always had," Paul whispered. "Oh my God, he could have even circled back and come in behind us." Paul whirled around looking behind him. "Damn, who's hunting who?" He turned back toward the basement and started forward again.

The sheriff saw the hand re-emerge. He waited... a little farther... a little more. He pounced, grabbing the hand. Paul was as tense as a jack-in-the-box waiting to spring. When the sheriff grabbed his hand, he sprung. The sheriff had one hand, and Paul's young limber body kept moving and squirming, keeping the sheriff from the motion he was trying for. Paul wildly swung his left fist at the sheriff, landing a glancing blow to his left eye. The sheriff had had enough and planted his knee in Paul's groin, caught Paul's head on his way down, and snapped his neck with precision. The sheriff moved Paul's body over to the right side of the landing next to Ned.

No blood and no bullets yet. So far, so good. The sheriff moved back to his position, waiting.

Vince had searched several rooms, including those already searched by Paul. He inched his way into the area where Ned had begun and entered the sheriff's bedroom. He looked around the room and his eyes settled on Max. "What the fuck? That crazy-ass sheriff has a damn stuffed dog sitting over there," Vince said to himself and turned toward the closet's open doors. Vince peeked inside the entrance and saw the bright light of the basement shining through the opening. "Weird shit going on around here. That's for sure," he muttered. He eased closer and closer.

The sheriff took a deep breath and exhaled slowly, and then another. He saw the end of a pistol sticking out of the entryway to the landing. *Deep, slow breath. Two down, two to go. Focus, Raymer. Stay in the moment.*

Vince eased forward again. He suddenly pulled his hand back, just as the sheriff went for it. The sheriff's hand grazed Vince's, startling him. Vince was in mid-jump when the sheriff appeared in front of him in a crouch.

"Son of a bitch!" Vince said, trying to get his feet to move. They didn't. The sheriff was on him. Vince's gun hand was secured. Twist and down. Vince was on the floor but managed to pull the trigger. The sound of the shot echoed through the house. From the floor, the sheriff swung hard with a wide, full arm extended chop to Vince's throat. His hand was on target, snapping Vince's windpipe. He jumped up, and dragged Vince to his friends. The sheriff heard Bert running in one of the other rooms, calling for Vince.

"Asshole, you put a damn bullet in my house," he whispered as he snapped Vince's neck to quiet his gasping. Then he moved back to his position by the door, waiting for the last one.

"Did you get him?" Bert yelled. There was no answer. "Ned... Paul... Vince, did you get him?" No answer. "Come on, guys, don't fuck with me... Vince," he yelled.

Bert stopped. He listened. "Why aren't they answering? The damn sheriff couldn't have taken out three men with guns." He was afraid to move forward. He was afraid to go back. He couldn't stay where he was.

The sheriff knew the next one would have the AK-47 and would be eager to use it. *Damn, I don't want my house shot up.* He waited, thinking. *This street-thug won't know what he's doing. He'll let the bolt slam forward instead of riding it, and I'll hear it unless he already has the bolt forward.* He heard the floor creak... another step. The sheriff knew he was in the bedroom now. Creak... he was checking the shower in the attached bathroom.

Bert saw the light coming from the closet. He moved toward it slowly. Without going through the entrance, he looked out onto the landing and beyond it, saw the basement. "Damn, what a set up," he mouthed the words. "He might be down there waiting. If he was gone, the others would be here answering me. He's gotta be in there. I should just get the fuck out of here. If I do, he'll still come looking for me. This is the best chance to get him. If I step through that door, he could shoot me. He doesn't have to be quiet anymore. The others didn't make a sound. Why didn't they? He surprised them. What if he's behind that wall? Huh, I can take care of that. I'll just kill his ass through the wall."

Bert eased closer, pulled his AK-47 in front of him. His hands were sweating as he quietly repeated the sequence, "release the bolt to slide forward, then move the selector lever from safe to semi or fully automatic fire. I'm going with fully automatic."

The sheriff heard the 'metallic microwave door slamming' sound of the bolt release, to chamber the round, and knew bullets would soon tear through the wall. Within a second, he had dropped flat onto the floor of the landing without a sound. In the two seconds that followed, he whistled sharply twice. In the next second, he heard the clicking sound similar to a metallic light switch being flipped. It was the selector lever moving from safe to semi or fully automatic fire. At the same time, Max sprang from his position toward Bert.

Max let Bert know he was coming with a snarling bark. Startled, Bert spun around and raised the AK-47 to kill Max. Bert was too late. Max jumped and pounced into

Bert's torso, pushing him backwards through the entrance to the landing. Bert, on the verge of falling backwards, kept stepping back with arms spread wide, trying to regain his balance and get away from the snarling, charging dog. He came to a sudden halt as he backed full speed into the landing safety rail. Diving for him, Max's two front feet landed full force on Bert's chest with just enough force to tip him over the rail. Bert fell twenty-five feet to the bottom of the basement, landing on a steel bar laid out on the concrete floor where the sheriff had begun work on a new set of shelves. The force of the fall onto the raised steel bar broke Bert's vertebrae just below his chest level. Dazed from hitting his head on the concrete, Bert slowly reached for the AK-47. It was about a half inch beyond the reach of his right hand. He stretched as far as he could trying to get it. His fingers barely touched the edge of it. He tried to move closer. He stretched a little more. The fingernail of his longest middle finger landed on the far side of the trigger guard. He began to pull at it. It moved toward him just a fraction of an inch.

Max turned, ran down the steps, and jumped the last five to the bottom. He loped toward his mark with every fiber of his being. He pounced once again onto Bert. This time, Max's mouth landed on Bert's throat, biting down with all his might. Bert's hand came up in a reflex action, trying to get the dog off him. He couldn't get any air through his windpipe. Max growled, bit even harder, and shook his head back and forth, burying his teeth deeper into Bert's neck.

The sheriff had gotten to his feet and walked down the stairs to the basement. He got to the bottom, turned to go to Bert, and stopped, noticing Bert's fixed stare. He was dead. The sheriff went to the other side of the room to the water well. He put a bucket under the hand pump and started pumping. When it was half full, he walked over to Max and Bert.

"Max, release," the sheriff said. Max let go. The sheriff sat on a nearby folding metal chair. "Max, come," the sheriff ordered. Max walked over to him.

"Good boy, Max. Good boy," the sheriff said. He put the bucket of water in front of Max who drank from it. The sheriff washed Max's mouth to remove any remaining blood. "Good boy, Max," the sheriff repeated. "You saved my ass, Maxie. Thank you." He petted Max and gave him a hug. "Come on, Maxie. Let's get out of here for a while." The sheriff put a plastic garbage bag topped by a towel under Bert's neck to catch the blood and went upstairs.

CHAPTER 33

Fires Burn in the Dark

I have to move that truck," Sheriff Raymer said to himself. He went to his closet and gathered an old raggedy pair of sweat pants and a sweat shirt. He put on a hair net and gloves and quickly changed into the sweats. He pulled plastic bags over his shoes and taped them at the top.

"Max, stay," the sheriff said. "Good boy." He thought as he walked out the front door, *I hope they left the keys in it. They probably wanted to leave fast. The keys are likely out here. I hope nobody heard that pistol go off.*

His home was over a mile away from his nearest neighbors in every direction, by his choice. He owned the land on both sides of the road, and right and left of the house for at least a mile. He didn't want to be bothered by neighbors. *Nobody would have heard the pistol unless they were trespassing.*

The keys were in the truck. He cranked it and drove down the driveway going to a large garage behind his home.

The land approaching the house was flat, but the house was built on a sharp slope. During the remodeling, the sheriff built a front-facing garage to the left of the house and added a door going into the house from the garage. He used this garage each day.

To the left of the new garage, the sheriff put a fork in the driveway that curved sharply left all the way to the fence, which surrounded the house and lawns. It also began a rapid descent as it curved to the backside of the house. Originally, there had been a set of stairs, a small porch, and a door on the back of the house going to the basement and the water well under the main living area of the house. Attached to the back of the house was a shelter for a tractor and other tools and equipment. The sheriff enclosed and upgraded the shelter into a huge garage with four large electronic doors.

The sheriff clicked the garage door opener. He turned the truck around as the door closest to the house opened. The sheriff got out of the truck and began a search of it. He pulled the seats up and looked under the dashboards. Under the passenger side floormat he found a hidden compartment filled with drugs and cash.

"Jackpot," said the sheriff. He pulled out wrapped bundles of cash and left the drugs. He backed the truck into the garage, parking it as close as possible to the back wall of the house. He exited the truck on the passenger side, jumped up into the back of the truck and clicked another automatic garage door opener. A section of the back wall of the house opened up. He stepped up onto the top of the side body of the truck bed. Standing on it, the concrete floor of the basement was level with his waist. He laid the bag of money on the basement floor and jumped up into the basement. He stashed the cash and then headed to the bodies.

The sheriff pulled together the ends of the plastic

garbage bag underneath the towel under Bert's head and neck and tied them in a knot. He went through Bert's pockets, removed the cash, and put his wallet in a plastic bag. Then he dragged him to the open door. He laid out a tarp in the bottom of the truck and dropped Bert into the truck. He poured some bleach on a small spot of blood and wiped it up with paper towel. Then he poured more bleach over it and left it puddled there.

The sheriff took a chain and went upstairs to the landing. Max barked from inside the bedroom. The sheriff opened the door and allowed Max to join him.

"Sit, Max. You can be here, buddy, but you've got to stay put. I don't want any of your hair showing up in that truck over there. Max, stay."

The sheriff systematically went through the pockets of the three men on the landing, saved the cash, and put their wallets in the plastic bag. He put the bloody paper towel in the bag with the wallets. The sheriff removed the safety bolts and swung a section of the landing safety rail open. One at a time, the sheriff fastened a chain underneath the arms of each man and attached it to the pulley system he had hanging from the rafters just beyond the railing of the landing. He lowered each into a waiting oversized wheel barrow and took them to the truck. He ushered Max back into the house and closed up the basement. The sheriff added three cans of gasoline from the garage and tied down a top tarp on the back of the truck.

Matches, gotta have some matches. He found a small box in a metal cabinet in the corner, tested them, and put them in his pocket.

"How am I going to get back?" he asked himself. He saw his motorcycle. "Too big, no way," he disqualified the idea. He saw his daughter's motor scooter in the corner. It had needed a new tire, which he had already replaced. He hadn't yet taken it back to her. Since she got her driver's license and a car, she rarely used it, but she and her girl-friends were all taking scooters with them to Panama City, Florida for spring break. Hers had a seat and a wire basket in back. He knew he'd look like an idiot on it, but it would get him home. *I'll use my tinted full-face helmet, so no one can see my face, and it'll be dark out by then anyway.* He checked its front and back lights. They were working. He put it in the truck.

At his grandfather's hunting property, the sheriff locked the gate behind him. He filled the bottom of the pit with logs, topped them with branches to allow air flow, and added more logs. He backed the truck up with the tailgate hanging over the edge of the burn pit and removed the bodies from the truck. He pulled it forward and unloaded the cans of gasoline. He knew this would have to be an incredible fire, burning hot for a long time to do what he needed.

He poured gasoline over each body and let it run into the bottom of the pit. He opened each man's wallet and threw in everything inside apart from the wallet, so it would be sure to thoroughly burn. He moved everything away from the pit. He got the water hose and wet down the sur-rounding area. The sheriff moved upwind from the burn pit, about fifteen feet away, lit a small pine branch, and threw it toward the pit.

After the initial roaring blaze, the fire settled down with the logs underneath doing their work. He moved to his chair and sat thinking. *Ned, Paul, Vince, and Bert, surely some-body's going to notice these scumbags are gone. I haven't heard a word about the first three being missing. I guess they don't have many friends.* After an hour, he added more logs to the fire. He also decided to throw the two tarps into the fire. *I'll buy new ones.*

He returned to his lawn chair. *I wonder how all these guys fell in with the likes of Carl Mitchell. He was scum but he had no problem telling them what to do and how great he was. They probably all wanted to make quick money and he offered that selling drugs. They all bought into his gang and pledged their allegiance to him. Carl made them prove their loyalty doing some bad stuff. They let that crazy nut make decisions for them and they just went along with him, like Charles Manson's group. Poor Paul. He was so young. The little decisions we make every day... they changes our lives.*

The sheriff sat sideways on the seat of the truck with his feet hanging outside. He removed the bags and tape he had on his feet, so none of the dirt from the pit area would get into the truck. He put what he'd removed into a fresh bag and laid it on the seat of the truck beside him. He re-bagged his shoes to deter shoe prints in the truck. The sun had gone down, and it was nearly dark now. He locked the gate on the way out of the property, leaving the fire to continue a slow burn and smolder overnight.

The sheriff drove to the Hide-a-Way Night Club where he had captured Oliver. It was just over the state line on the Georgia side of the river. It was completely dark now. The big black King Cab truck he drove had Georgia tags on it. He saw an empty parking place between two other trucks. He took it. He lowered the windows and unlocked all four doors. He left the keys in the ignition. He leaned over into the passenger side, popped the lid on the hidden compartment underneath the floormat, and took out the drugs. He put the floormat back in place. He pulled a few of the drugs out of the bag, positioned them on the passenger seat, and put a few on the dash board. There was a loose twenty-dollar bill in the bag. He put it on the dash board to draw attention and turned on the interior passenger-side light. The sheriff unloaded the scooter from the back seat and wiped down the seats and back floormats. He put on his dark tinted, full face helmet, and peeked out to see if anyone was around before pulling out from between the two big trucks on the scooter. He drove by the dumpster and tossed in the bag with the rest of the drugs.

The sheriff waited at the main highway until he saw nothing coming from either direction. As soon as he cleared the bridge over the Muscogee River, he took the first road, getting him off the highway and onto Riverside Road. A little farther down, he turned beside three silos onto Parrish Road. A smaller, less traveled road running parallel to Riverside Road. It would get him home and keep him safe from traffic.

❖❖❖

"Hey, Maxie, there's my buddy," the sheriff said. He petted and fed Max. Then he lit a fire in his fireplace. He threw in his hair net, gloves, the bag, and then his sweatshirt and pants. He showered and then invited Max to ride with him in his truck to pick up takeout food.

Later that night, he watched the fire in his fireplace, and made plans for what he needed to do out at the fire pit. Then he mentally reviewed everything, trying to determine if he had missed some tiny detail or piece of evidence that might one day haunt him.

CHAPTER 34

On the Muscogee

Good morning. Are you ready for our day cruise steamboat adventure?" Jack asked as he leaned in for a hug and a kiss.

"I'm ready," Angelica said. "Do you think I'll need a jacket?"

"Yes, bring it just in case. The weather's supposed to be sunny all day, but there will be a lot of wind on the boat deck."

"I'm so excited. I've never been on a steamboat before," Angelica said. "Is this a steamboat or a paddle wheeler boat?"

"The one we're going on is both," Jack said. "A steamboat, some people call it a **steamship or steamer,** is a ship that uses a steam engine to move it. Way back, they were paddle steamboats. Some had a paddle wheel on the back and others had two wheels on the sides. Ours has a paddle wheel in the back. The steam engine makes the paddles turn around which propels the ship."

"Where do we get on the boat?" Angelica asked. They

were driving out of River Rock, heading north on Riverside Road.

"The dock is up at Jasmine Point. That's where we'll board. It's not too far. I've always liked driving along this road and watching the river twist and turn. Where did you grow up, Angelica?"

They talked as they drove along and soon reached their destination.

"Look at it. It's beautiful," Angelica said, seeing the steamboat. "Let's get a picture." She'd brought her camera and a passing teenager took several pictures of them together and with them in front of the steamboat. The boat's whistle blew, and they boarded the boat.

"I'm so excited. I don't know if I can sit still," Angelica said and did a little happy dance in front of Jack.

"Well, then let's walk around the outer railings a few laps and burn off a little steam." Jack snickered.

Angelica snapped pictures of everything. On the far side of the boat, they paused, looking out over the river.

"Look over there. What is that?" She zoomed in with her camera. "It's otters! There are otters playing near the far bank." She had him look through her camera to see them.

A steam powered organ began to play the song, *Old Suzanna*, and then, *Dixieland*, and more.

"This is so much fun," Angelica said. "Thank you for bringing me here."

"We haven't even left the dock yet," Jack said. He smiled at her, thinking how easy it was for her to be happy and enjoy herself and wishing he could be more like her. *How light her spirit is. How sweet she is.*

"Good morning, ladies and gentlemen. This is Captain Rod Daniels. We're happy to have you with us today. I hope you all will relax and enjoy the beautiful landscapes as we make our way along the Muscogee River. We'll be departing from Port Jasmine Point and traveling up river to the city and port of Merrieville. We will make a stop there and a second stop to explore Berry Hill Plantation and her captivating gardens, ponds, and ancient oak trees. You'll see that Berry Hill Plantation is rich in beauty and history. Lunch will be provided while you're at the plantation."

Traveling up the river, Jack and Angelica found seats on the outside deck. Jack helped her slip her jacket on and then held her from behind as they both watched each new scene with each bend of the river. With his arms around her, he leaned his head down, "I could get used to this."

"Me too," she said, looking up at him. She turned to him, and they kissed. They sat in lounge chairs on the deck, holding hands. He felt the warm connection between them, something he had been without for many years, something he had nearly forgotten existed. He found it soothing.

"Are you taking me to church tomorrow, Jack?" she asked.

"Yes, ma'am, I am," he said. She smiled.

"I'll be ready," she said.

"Look, I believe I see Huck Finn and Tom Sawyer on that raft over there."

"My goodness," she said. "Look at the top of that tree up there. I really do see an eagle's nest. Do you see it?"

At church the next morning, Senator Billy and his family were already seated when Jack and Angelica took their seats across the aisle.

"Do you know him?" Angelica asked, nodding toward Billy. "He was looking at you just now."

"He was probably looking at you, the beautiful one." They smiled at one another.

"Yes, I know him. Billy and I both grew up here. We went to school together. Then I joined the Marines and was away a good bit for the next twenty years, so it's not like we've spent much time together through the years. Do you want to meet him?"

"Yes," she said.

After the pastor's sermon, the music director led the congregation in, *Just as I Am*. Jack felt the strange stirrings and pull to pray at the altar. The feeling had now become somewhat familiar to him. The pastor said it was the Holy Ghost. He hadn't decided on what, or who, he would call or name it. He yielded to it and went to pray. After the pastor's closing prayer, before going to stand by the front door as everyone departed, he turned to Jack.

"Jack, if you ever want to come to my office during the week to talk or pray together, feel free. I'm here most of the time, and everything said is completely confidential," Pastor Stevenson said.

"Thank you, Pastor. I appreciate it. I'll keep that in mind."

Billy looked up and nodded at Jack. Jack threw up his hand to flag Billy, who then allowed himself to smile at the sheriff and move toward him.

"Billy, someone wants to meet you." Jack reached out for Angelica and introduced her to Billy. The senator introduced her to his wife and children. Billy squeezed his wife's hand and looked to Angelica.

"Angelica, I would love to know you better. Would you and Jack like to come to dinner sometime at our home?" Mrs. Bradford asked.

"I'd love to," Angelica said.

"I'll call you later, and we'll make a date," Mrs. Bradford told her.

They made their way outside. The women were in front, chatting.

"You're still after that photo for the Hispanic vote, aren't you, Billy?"

"Why, Jack, what a great idea. It never entered my mind." He laughed. "I'm glad to see the two of you have gotten together. She seems like a nice person. She might be good for you, Jack."

"I think she's going to be very good for me," Jack said.

CHAPTER 35

My Box

Sitting in his chair in the dark, Sheriff Raymer stared at the flickering and flashing, light and dark, of the television screen broadcasting the late-night news. It was muted. He could hardly stand to watch it, but he couldn't stay away. Max walked in, whined, and pulled Jack's shirt tail.

"Time for bed, huh? I know, buddy. I'll be there in a little bit. Go. You go ahead," he urged. Max let go and left the room. Five minutes later, Max was back, whining and staring with pleading eyes.

"Not now, Maxie. I'm thinking. Go." Max laid his chin on Jack's knee. Jack rubbed Max's head. Max stepped up into the chair with his two front feet, getting closer. "Need a little attention, boy? I think I know that feeling." Max stepped up into the chair with his back feet, standing above the sheriff. "Max, Max, you're too big to sit on my lap." Undeterred, Max laid on Jack's lap and closed his eyes. "Maxie, you've put on some weight, buddy. Can't you sleep without me? I know, it's nicer with someone, huh?" Jack rubbed and massaged Max.

"Maxie, I've been spending time with a lady. Her name is Angelica. Isn't that pretty? It suits her. She's beautiful. I doubt it'll ever happen, but if she ever comes home with me, and we make it all the way to the bedroom, you'll have to find somewhere else to sleep. I'm telling you now, so if it happens, don't act like you didn't know." He laughed.

"Angelica has me going to church, Max. Do you believe that? It's been a long time for me since I went regularly. Last week, one of the members told me after church, she and her Sunday School class members have been talking about how 'proud they are that Clayborne County has such a praying sheriff, who loves the Lord.' You could have knocked me over with a feather. If she knew what I pray about every Sunday that rolls, she might not have been singing my praises." Max opened his eyes, made a long, happy sigh, and promptly closed them again.

"Maxie, I can't figure out if I'm a good guy or a bad guy. I wonder what God thinks I am. That's what I pray about. When I joined the Marines, I didn't have a clue what it would be like to fight in a war. I doubt any of us first-timers did. I got over there to Kosovo and Bosnia and what a shock. Things got real, fast. Buddy, there were people dying left and right in our unit. We had become friends and then, there they were right in front of me, being shot or getting blown up, into pieces, literally. I knew it could have been me. We knew anybody over there might kill us. We kept deploying to stay with our unit, and then one day, we looked around and 90% of our unit had been killed. Do you believe that? I could hardly believe it and every day I thought, 'This might be the day I die too.'

"Maxie, I killed a lot of people. I killed young men I didn't even know and personally didn't have a beef with, and they were like me, killing us for reasons they probably didn't know. We had so much adrenaline pumping over there that we'd hear the slightest sound and whirl around, ready to kill. We had that 'kill or be killed' mentality going… on steroids.

"Sometimes we fought day and night. There were days we didn't get to eat or sleep. When we were in the middle of it, our prayers were always, 'Please God, don't let the ammo run out before the next ammo drop comes.' If it did, we knew we'd all be goners.

"When we'd finally get home on leave, we were supposed to act normal, like we did before going there, like none of that nightmare had ever happened. We were supposed to act like our friends and family, who might be talking about what a horrible time they were having with their boss or wife or girlfriend, or how they just couldn't find the right pair of shoes. Oh, and when somebody sneaked up behind us to surprise us, oh my God, we weren't supposed to kill them.

"When we got home, to be anywhere close to normal, we had to put all of our combat-time mental baggage into a box and put it on a shelf. I did that and always hoped I could lose the box forever. Then I'd redeploy and would need all that boxed up stuff so I could keep killing, and to keep from dying, so I'd open it back up.

"Maxie, I've been trying to figure things out. A man can kill all those people in Afghanistan, people he doesn't even know. He fights because the American people told him to go there and kill people, that's the mission. And I was just telling Senator Billy, that the same guy comes home and if he kills the man who raped his little girl, then he's going to prison for the rest of his life or to the electric chair. I can't figure it out. I can't wrap my brain around it. I think about it, and it boggles my mind.

"I've been home for over five years, Maxie… I think I've

opened my combat box. I think maybe that's what I did every time I went after one of those guys that raped Emma, Billy, and me. And now… now I pray to God, every Sunday, that I can keep the lid on my box closed. And I pray that I keep it locked. And that I'll lose it one day.

"See how fucked-up I am, Maxie, and I'm one of those who supposedly has it all together. Maybe that's why so many of us blow our brains out when we get home. I guess I've thought about it. But don't worry Maxie, that's not something I'll ever do. You'll have me here as long as you can stand me, buddy. How could I leave you, my family, and friends with suicide as my legacy? That's all they would remember about me. Even if I don't have anyone who cares about me, I know I still make a difference and help people. Sometimes it's people that no one else would bother to help. Those are the ones I most like helping. I'll be here Maxie, and I'll face whatever comes my way."

CHAPTER 36

Roofing

C areful, honey," Sheriff Raymer called out to Angelica. She was carrying a water hose. Jack was pressure washing Old Jake Dawsey's house. She insisted she would join him to help out if she could and was repositioning the hose as he moved around the house. After moving it, she joined Old Jake who had a glass of lemonade waiting for her under an oak tree.

Jack wanted Angelica to know what he was planning for the next two Saturdays so she would understand why he wasn't asking her to spend Saturday time with him. He wanted to do the pressure wash ahead of the group work day, so everything could dry out before the big day. He was pleased when she wanted to come along.

She took a seat in one of the Adirondack chairs. "This is marvelous lemonade. What brand is it?"

Laughing, Jake Dawsey said, "That's Old Jake's home-made lemonade."

"It's delicious. Would you share your recipe with me?"

"They ain't no recipe, ma'am. But I will let you watch me make it some time. If you want to, you can set it down on paper."

"Thank you," Angelica said. "I'd like that. Have you known Sheriff Raymer a long time, Mr. Dawsey?"

"Just call me Old Jake, everybody does. Yes'm, in a way I've known him a long time. My boy John went to high school with the sheriff. They were on the same football team. Sheriff Raymer defended my boy one day and made some white boys leave him alone. They never bothered him again. That's how I first knew of Jack Raymer."

"So, he's been a good guy for a long time then. That's good to know."

"Yes'm. He's a good man. I expect you could do a lot worse than him."

The pressure washing went smoothly and didn't take long because the house was small.

"The truck with the supplies is supposed to deliver here on Thursday," the sheriff said. "I gave them your phone number. The driver is supposed to call when he gets close, so you can show him where to unload." He and Old Jake talked about where would be the best place to unload and how the truck might back into the area.

Angelica went back to Jack's house with him. He said he'd take her for a late lunch or early dinner but wanted a shower first. She was interested to see his house.

"Angelica, meet Max. Max, this is Angelica, the one I told you about."

"You told him about me?"

"Yes, I did. Just in case you showed up here one day."

Jack laughed. He showed her around the house, told her it was over a hundred years old and named off a few of the remodeling projects he'd done. He invited her to look around or visit with Max while he had a quick shower. She looked around the house, the huge back deck built over the four-door garage, and the back yard. She and Max meandered back toward Jack's room. He was out of the shower, wearing only pants.

"There you are. I'm glad you didn't leave," Jack said.

She moved to him. "I'm not going anywhere." She smiled. "Your back is wet. Here, let me dry it for you." She reached for the towel and moved it over the droplets. He turned around. She dabbed at droplets across is muscular chest and arms. She smelled his antiperspirant and the cologne he'd just put on after his touch-up shave. She moved closer to him and kissed his chest. He hugged her. The feel of his skin against her made her want him. He could feel it. He kissed her, and then again, and then with urgency and passion. She returned it, but then pushed him back a bit.

"Jack, stop. We should go."

"Angelica, maybe we should stay." He nuzzled her neck.

"I want to, Jack. You turn me on, but I'm not quite ready. I'm sorry. I want it to mean something special. Let's wait awhile and get to know each other better."

"Umm." He still nuzzled. He moved to her lips and kissed her again, gently. "Angelica, I know. I love you. There's something about you, inside you that captured my heart the first time you smiled, looked into my eyes, and told me, 'Good Morning.' I want you. Not just here in my bedroom, but in my life. I feel connected to you in a warm and satisfying way that I can't explain. I want to marry you, Angelica, but I know it's too soon for a sensible woman like you to say 'yes,' but please don't say 'no.' Don't say anything. Just know that I love you, and if one day you feel like you know me well enough, and you love me too, I'll be here, waiting for you."

"Jack, I don't know what to say. So much of what you said, I feel too."

"Encouragement is good. I'll take it." So, let's get something to eat. I'll put on my shirt, because if you keep touching my nipples like that, I don't think I'll be able to control myself much longer." He laughed, and she did too.

"Billy, what's our bill with your brother-in-law for the roofing materials?" Sheriff Raymer asked the following week. Senator Billy pulled out the ticket on it for Jack to review.

"I've got some donations here. I gave Angelica $300 to get food, snacks, and drinks for everyone for the day. Here's the rest," said the sheriff. He had Carl Mitchell's $2,500 and $5,300 from the paper sack in Oliver's truck.

"You did great, Jack," Senator Billy said. "I thought you were going to stick me with the whole bill. It's all cash? What, didn't people want a receipt or to use a check as their record of a charitable donation?"

"I'm not a 501(c)(3), Billy. I don't give any receipts. You did a great job getting us the materials for cost, and it's a small roof. After taking out the $300, there's $7,500 left. I'll give you the cost listed on the ticket, and me the amount for the paint and brushes, and there'll be a little left over. I'm going to put that on a prepaid Visa card for Old Jake to use however he wants."

"Fine by me," said Billy. "Let's get this show on the road. You don't mind if I paint with the girls instead of climbing up on the roof, do you?"

"That's fine, Billy. You'll need to be down here anyway

for when the press gets here." Jack laughed. "What a blue-sky beautiful day for working outside."

Angelica took the girls who volunteered from the high school and went inside the house where they covered everything to protect it when the old roof was being torn off and replaced. Jack took the high school boys with him. The professional roofer from the church was their official foreman and explained what they would be doing. Two other men from church came to help, as well.

After things in the house were covered, Angelica's team painted the exterior. They were to work on the opposite side of the house from where the men were working, and basically work around them.

Millie Watson was one of the girl volunteers. She and Ray Raymer sat on the porch together during each break time, snacking on macadamia nut cookies Millie had baked the night before for him. She and Ray had been dating ever since his apology.

The sheriff was pleased to have his son helping and learning about roofing, but he was also happy his daughter, Julie, came to help. The sheriff noticed she and one of the boys spent some time talking during the breaks. He later learned the boy's name was not Zack.

The television crew showed up, and Senator Billy got the publicity he needed for his campaign. Billy also mentioned that Sheriff Raymer had organized the project.

After the new metal roof was on and the house was painted, things were uncovered inside. Then Angelica's team swept the floors and porches, and everyone started to leave. Old Jake took Angelica back inside and showed her how he made his lemonade. She waited in the truck, drinking iced lemonade from a red plastic cup, while the sheriff went to say goodbye to Old Jake.

"Sheriff, you didn't have to do any of this, and I don't rightly know why you did, but I want you to know I'm glad for it. Thank you, sir."

"You're welcome, Jake. I'm happy to help. You know my parents passed a long time ago. I'll count helping you as helping them. Call me if you need me."

"I remember when that happened, a house fire as I recall, a terrible tragedy it was. Bless your heart, you were just a youngster. I don't know how you could've lived through the fire and losing both parents. I'm glad your grandfather was there for you."

CHAPTER 37

The Article

It was Saturday, and Noah was at the sheriff's office, putting in a few hours of volunteer time on his special project. He had gathered hundreds of last names for his lists of first names, along with other bits of data for each listed. He had just gone through and prioritized each list, filtering the lists by those towns and cities closest to River Rock.

The sheriff didn't tell Noah what case these names were connected to and had forbidden him to make assumptions, but Noah felt like these names had to do with Emma's rapists. He knew there were seven rapists, and the sheriff had given him five names. He wondered if Emma had only been able to remember five names or if only five names had been mentioned in her presence. Feeling like he was working to catch Emma's rapists had made him eager to come back to work week after week.

Noah had worked through each idea he'd come up with for gathering names. He sat thinking, trying to imagine anything else he might try, what might help in any way.

What if I do searches for all of the first names together in different internet search engines? Yeah, whether these are Emma's bad guys or even if they have nothing to do with Emma, they must be connected in some way for the sheriff to have put them together on a list. What if they have been connected in a way, public enough, to have made it onto the internet? It's worth a try, isn't it? Yes, good idea, Noah.

Noah went online and typed the five first names into the search field of the default search engine on the computer. He searched through all the pages of hits that popped up, looking for anything that might be something. After thirty minutes of looking and reading, he switched to a different search engine, still hoping. He worked through two other search engines' listings and then decided to change the search by adding 'Alabama' at the end of the search data. A half hour later, Noah deleted 'Alabama' and added 'Georgia' in the search.

The first item up on the results list was a newspaper article from Shorterville, Georgia, a city just across the Muscogee River from River Rock. Noah's heart beat faster. He saw right away, all five of the names listed in the article and one more, Carl Mitchell. He had stopped breathing, and suddenly took a gasping breath. *Oh my God! This has got to be them!* He read the article.

Oh my God! I wonder if the sheriff has seen this. What if he already knows?

"What are you doing, Mom?" Noah asked.

"I'm fixing your sister's plate for you to take to her, so we can have supper."

"Mom, please. Could Emma eat with us tonight? I'll lock

the front door. I have something I want to talk about, and I'd like Emma to be here for it."

"My goodness, a mystery. Well, you make it sound important. All right. Be sure to close the front blinds too."

"Mom, really, Emma's not even showing yet."

"Yes, she is, a tiny bit now.

❖❖❖

They were all seated, the blessing was asked, and their plates were filled. Things seemed awkward. Emma had always been the family peacekeeper, the one who smoothed out awkward moments and pulled them all together. But tonight, Emma hadn't said a word, nor had her parents. They had all been eating in silence when Noah assumed Emma's role and said, "I have a date for the ball-game next week."

"You didn't ask about taking a girl out, and we haven't met her," Gayle said. "Is that the big news you wanted Emma to be here for?"

"No, ma'am," Noah said. "It's just a ballgame, Mom. There will be hundreds of other people there.

"I wanted to tell you all, at the same time, about something I came across on the internet today. I'm not really supposed to talk about it, but it might involve Emma, so I think I should."

"What in the world are you talking about?" Gayle asked.

"Sheriff Raymer gave me five names to do research on when I first started volunteering at his office. He wouldn't tell me anything about the names or why he wanted information on them. He told me not to assume anything, but I always wondered if it had something to do with Emma's case. I've been working on it for a while and today I did a search, including all the names, which turned up a news article from a paper in Shorterville. I printed it out. I'll read it to you."

"Isn't this interesting? The sheriff gave me all these names weeks ago except for one, Carl Mitchell. Now they have all gone missing. Emma, are these the names of the

THE SHORTERVILLE GAZETTE

Public Assistance Requested in Missing Men Case

By Bill Watson

Investigators report no leads in missing men case. Police Chief, Phil Ready of Shorterville, Georgia stated, "We have no leads nor persons of interest in the case of the six missing men. We ask the public to call in tips and anything noticed out of the ordinary concerning these men. The men range in age from 22 to 29. Their names are: Carl Mitchell, Bert Taylor, Vince Kelley, Ned Collins, Oliver Banner, Paul Malcomb. All live in and around Shorterville, Georgia. It is unclear as to the exact dates the men disappeared. Investigations have been hampered by lack of facts in the case.

What we know: None of the men work at public jobs. All appear to be friends with one another. All drive motorcycles regularly. None of the men are married, and none keep in close contact with family members. This has made pinpointing the exact time of their disappearances impossible, thus far. Please contact the police department with any information.

men who hurt you?" Noah asked.

Emma was white as a sheet. She sat perfectly still, staring at the roast beef on her plate. She said nothing.

"Well, maybe the sheriff made them disappear or something," said Noah.

"You've been watching too many murder mysteries," Emma said.

"No, he has a point," Gayle said. "It sounds very suspicious to me. We'll have to report this to higher authorities. He can't be taking the law into his own hands like that."

"That's ridiculous! The sheriff would never do that. He's a good man. You should leave him alone. You don't have to report anything." Emma got louder as she spoke.

"Well, if we have information to report, we need to report it. And don't you speak to me in that tone of voice, young lady," Gayle said.

Gabe, as usual, sat silent, watching and listening. No one expected him to say anything, but he did.

"'Judge not, sayeth the Lord,' that's what our Bible says," Gabe said quietly. Everyone turned to look at him.

"Anything the sheriff did or didn't do is between him and God, and it's not for any of us to judge him. Just because any of us suspects he might have had something to do with the disappearance of those men, that doesn't mean he did. Those men are bad men and probably into a lot of bad and illegal things. Even the article says none of them have jobs, so they must be getting their money illegally. Any one of their colleagues or rival groups could have done away with them all. There's no use in damaging the sheriff's reputation or career because any of us have a suspicion, especially when not a one of us has any evidence to back it up. I'm the man of this house, and I'll not have us reporting any unfounded suspicions about Sheriff Raymer to anyone.

"What's more, if he did do it, then I say, the good Lord works through man in mysterious ways, that the sheriff in his own way is just keeping our daughter and the other women of this city safe, and, Gayle, if you disrespect me by saying a word to anyone about this, especially the authorities, I will no longer live here with you!"

"You don't mean that!"

"I meant every word I said, and I'll do just exactly what I said."

"If you leave, I'm going with you, Daddy," Emma said.

"Emma!"

"I'll go too," Noah said.

"Now, Gayle, this is one subject you're to remain quiet on, from now forward. You are not to speak of, nor disparage the sheriff to anyone, or in anyway, now or in the future. Do you understand me?"

She lowered her head, exhaled, and said, "Yes, Gabe."

Emma smiled at Noah and then her father, who winked at her.

"Please pass the mashed potatoes," Emma said. Noah handed them over.

"Son, you and your girlfriend have fun at the ballgame," Gabe said.

"Thank you, Dad," Noah said.

"Yes, thank you, Daddy," Emma said.

CHAPTER 38

The Rocket Center

Where's your brother?" Sheriff Jack Raymer asked Julie, as he put her suitcase in the trunk of his car.

"He's asleep. He's not going. He doesn't care anything about science or space and decided to stay home. I think he has a date tonight too, with Millie," Julie said.

"Well, we don't want to interfere with that. I guess it's just me and you then," said Jack. They were going to Huntsville to the U.S. Space and Rocket Center. He read about it when he thought of inviting Julie for the trip. He had never been and thought it would be interesting.

Sarah came outside to see them off. "Have a good time and be careful," she said.

"You're going to feed and water Max, aren't you?"

"Yes, I haven't forgotten. I'll take care of him."

"Max is outside. The food is in the cabinet on the back deck. I put the hose on the faucet to make it easier. Thanks for seeing after him. Don't get too cozy with him. I'll pout if he loves you more than me, you know."

"Yes, I know you will." She laughed. "Be safe," she called as they pulled away.

They picked up coffee, Cajun chicken biscuits, and strawberry jelly, and headed to the highway.

"I've been looking forward to this ever since I asked you about going," Jack said. "I think it'll be fun. I hope you'll like it."

"I'm sure I will, Daddy."

"Did you look it up online to read about it?"

"No, I meant to, but never did," Julie said.

"Open my laptop when you're finished eating, if you want to read about it. I've got information saved from their website queued up on the Space Center. The Huntsville Botanical Garden is right beside the Space Center. While we're in the area, we can tour there too, if you want."

Julie pulled out the laptop and read. "The U.S. Space & Rocket Center in Huntsville, Alabama is a museum operated by the state of Alabama, showcasing rockets, achievements, and artifacts of the U.S. space program. Some call it Earth's largest space museum. It showcases Apollo Program hardware, has interactive science exhibits, videos, and space simulators."

"That sounds like a lot to see," said Jack.

"There's loads more listed here," Julie said.

"It'll take awhile to get there, but I'm glad we're going," he said.

"So, you said you'd answer questions while we're riding," Julie reminded him.

"I did say that, and I see your memory is working fine."

"Okay, here goes the first one. Hypothetically, if I've been seeing someone for a long time and he's nice sometimes, but some other times, he's not so nice, or he says things that hurt my feelings, should I stick with him, hoping he will change?"

"Does he know he's saying or doing things that hurt your

feelings?" Jack asked. "Does he understand what he's doing wrong and why it's wrong?"

"Yes, he does. I've been very clear about it."

"Bravo for you. You've been clear, and you're not giving him mixed messages. You have consistently and clearly spoken or shown him that whatever he did or said isn't all right with you. Some people act upset sometime but then at other times, they blow it off, don't say anything, and might even try to kiss or cuddle to make the person acting badly, happy again, and the bad guy gets rewarded for acting badly. See what I mean?"

"I see, Daddy, but I've always been mad and acted that way when I've been treated badly."

"Good girl, I'm proud you stand up for yourself in that way."

Julie smiled.

"Dump him," said Jack bluntly. "If you've done all that and he doesn't care enough to change his behavior, then he doesn't deserve you, and you definitely do not deserve to be treated that way. You've given him an opportunity to change, and he hasn't taken it. Dump him.

"There is someone else out there who will treat you with dignity and respect, and if he accidentally hurts your feelings, and you let him know, he will be deeply sorry, and he'll not do that same thing again. That's the guy for you."

"Wow, when you say it like that, it makes sense. When I'm around him, things get fuzzy, and I don't know what to do."

"Saying something is always easier than doing it. But after you say it in your mind a few times, it gets easier to do. Think about it."

"I will, Daddy, thanks."

"You remember Betty and Jerry from the Rape Crisis

Center. They're always looking for volunteers to help them. They have a lot of brochure racks there. You might go by and put the brochures out in the racks for them once each week. That would help them out, and you could look at all the brochures. They have more than sexual assault brochures. They have some on domestic violence and other forms of mental, physical, and verbal abuse. They're interesting to read. I've read a lot of them."

"I'll stop by there," Julie said.

They toured the Botanical Gardens that afternoon, and the next day were at the Space Center. Pictures were taken of them in front of a green screen before they entered the museum. Before leaving, Jack bought a package of photos where they had been patched into various backgrounds. They saw the Space Shuttle and Army rocketry and aircraft with more than fifteen hundred permanent rocketry and space exploration artifacts. The Apollo 16 capsule was on display, with the recovery parachute hanging above it. They saw a restored engineering mockup of Skylab and much more.

"Daddy, listen to this. 'This is the resting place of Miss Baker, a squirrel monkey who flew on a test flight of the Jupiter rocket in 1959. She lived at the Center from 1971 to 1984. She died of kidney failure.' She was a celebrity monkey."

They spent most of the day at the Space Center and decided to stay a second night before driving home. They went out to supper at a lovely restaurant, talking easily with one another as though Jack had never been absent from Julie's life.

Jack noticed Julie didn't ask the other question she had mentioned earlier. "Why didn't you treat Mom better?"

CHAPTER 39

The Talk

Hey, Julie," Noah said. "Do you need some help with those?" Julie and some of her friends were handing out brochures to students as they entered the auditorium. Julie had gone by the Rape Crisis Center as her father had suggested and had become a once per week volunteer. She sorted and stocked brochures in the big display racks at the center. She had taken most of them home to read, bringing them back the following week. Betty Jackson, the director of the center, asked her to hand out brochures for today's school assembly. Julie enlisted a few friends to help out so every entrance would be covered.

"Hey, Noah, we've got all the doors covered. Thanks, though," Julie said.

"I've been volunteering some at the sheriff's office with your dad. He's been great to me."

"Really? So, you like hanging out with him? Wow." Julie raised her eyebrows.

"Yeah, he's helped me with some things. I like your dad... you know, as much as a teenager can like being around a grown up." Noah laughed, trying to make light of his comments.

"I guess he's okay," Julie said. "For a long time, I didn't see much of him, but he's been coming around more lately. I guess he's trying. I just don't want him trying to tell me what to do or who I should or shouldn't date."

"I can understand that. See you later, Julie."

Nancy, Noah's girlfriend, was waiting just inside the auditorium. He reached out for her hand. She smiled. Sheriff Raymer walked up the aisle and spoke to Noah, who introduced him to Nancy. The sheriff winked at Noah as he and Nancy left to find seats.

Ray Raymer and Millie came down the aisle. "Hey, Dad, you remember Millie, don't you?"

"Yes, I do. How are you?" the sheriff asked.

"Fine, sir, and you?" Millie replied.

"I'm doing well. It's nice to see you again. Ray, I know it's hard to have your old man speaking at your school. I hope I don't embarrass you."

"Don't worry about it, Dad. I'm a Raymer. I can take it," Ray said.

"What do you think, son? Do you think it's all right for me to skip the chitchat and be brutally blunt about the facts?"

"Straightforward is good, Dad. That's what we need. No need to beat around the bush about anything. We'll see you later. We better find our seats."

"Okay, son. I'm glad I got to see you." Ray and Millie turned to go. "Ray," said the sheriff and Ray turned back to his father. "I love you, son."

"I love you too, Dad."

❖❖❖

Principal Fred Stevens asked for quiet and then introduced Betty and Jerry Jackson, counselors from the Rape Crisis Center. Betty Jackson was to be the first speaker. At sixty-three years old, she could have been the students' grand-mother. She had snow-white hair and was very trim, making her look a little frail. When Betty spoke into the microphone, there was no doubt she was a strong woman, with strong feelings about rape and sexual assault.

"I'm grateful to have this opportunity to talk with you today," Betty Jackson said. "I understand many of you may not have taken part in this type of training before. You may not have had conversations with your parents about sex, rape, or sexual abuse. Many of you might feel embarrassed. You might prefer to ignore and not hear about these topics. I think knowing about things that happen, at an alarming rate, to people in your age group is monumentally important.

"To illustrate what I mean, from 2009-2013, every eight minutes, Child Protective Services agencies substantiated, or found strong evidence to indicate that 63,000 children a year were victims of sexual abuse. Of all the victims under age eighteen, 66% were ages twelve to seventeen, and 34% under age twelve.

"I'm sure you all know what rape is. It's generally putting your penis..." the room erupted in laughter at the mention of penis. "All right, I guess I surprised you with that word. But rape is putting your penis or an object inside someone else without his or her permission. If the other person is incapacitated, they cannot give their consent. There are different crimes based on ages and what is done. You can ask the sheriff, when he speaks, to go into detail about that if you want to know which gets you more prison time.

"I want you to understand how often and where this happens, and who is most likely to do it. We will give you some statistics on it. Children are included in these numbers because you have all been children and, I dare say, some of you have been sexually assaulted or raped already. You may have never told anyone about it.

"If you want to talk to any of the speakers after this program is over, we will all be here for that purpose and your principal has said it will be all right.

"The statistics and information about RAINN you'll hear today, all comes from the RAINN website. If you want to know where they get their numbers, go to their websites www.rainn.org and www.rainn.org/es where they have it listed. Their National Sexual Assault Hotline phone number is: 800-656-HOPE (4673).

"RAINN stands for: Rape, Abuse & Incest National Network. It is said to be 'the nation's largest anti-sexual violence organization.' RAINN created and operates their hotline and websites 'in partnership with more than a thousand local sexual assault service providers across the country and operates the DoD Safe Helpline for the Department of Defense. RAINN also carries out programs to prevent sexual violence, help survivors, and ensure that perpetrators are brought to justice.

"'Every ninety-eight seconds, an American is sexually assaulted. And every eight minutes, that victim is a child. Meanwhile, only six out of every thousand perpetrators will end up in prison.

"'The number of people victimized *each year* by category are:

- General Public: 321,500 Americans twelve and older sexually assaulted or raped.

- Children: 63,000 victims of 'substantiated or indicated' sexual abuse.
- Inmates: 80,600 sexually assaulted or raped.
- Military: 18,900 experienced unwanted sexual contact.

"'Men, women, and children are all affected by sexual violence. One out of every six American women, and one in thirty-three men, have been the victim of an attempted or completed rape in their lifetime.

"'One in nine girls and one in fifty-three boys under the age of eighteen experience sexual abuse or assault at the hands of an adult.

"'82% of all victims under eighteen are female. Females ages sixteen to nineteen are four times more likely than the general population to be victims of rape, attempted rape, or sexual assault.'

"This shows you the magnitude of what's going on in our country, and sadly, it goes on here in our city and county too. Our next speaker is Mrs. Teresa Smith, who will tell you some of her personal experiences."

"Hello, I'm Teresa Smith and I'm one of those statistics. I came here today because I don't want any of you to stay in a situation where you're being sexually abused. I don't want you to blame yourself, if you're being abused. I want you to know that better can be had. I spent years blaming myself for something that wasn't my fault and being terrified and ashamed.

"When I was six years old, there was an old man who exposed his privates to me. He lived down the street from my family. I had a bicycle and often rode it up and down our street. We lived in a cul-de-sac. The old man started giving me candy so I would stop and talk with him. He pretended to be my friend. One day, he said he had baked cookies, and I should go inside with him to get one. They were chocolate chip which were my favorite. He had asked me my favorite cookie during one of our earlier talks. He said he had ice cream for me, to go with the cookies, if I was a good girl. I was sitting in his kitchen, when he exposed his erect penis to me. I had never seen anything like it and was scared. I knew I wasn't supposed to be seeing this. I wasn't allowed in the bathroom with my father or brothers. He told me to be a good girl and tried to grab me, but I flew home. I hid in my room. When Momma came to get me, I told her what he had done, and I was sent back to my room while she and Daddy talked about it. They sounded angry and upset. I thought I had been bad for going in his house and seeing what I saw. No one ever talked about it again. I buried my fear and my shame and tried to avoid seeing the old man down the street. I learned early not to trust, and my parents taught me not to tell.

"When I was fourteen, in the eighth grade, I stayed after school. I was at the football field. My older brother had football practice. He was fifteen. I sat in the bleachers, watching the cheerleaders practice. I fantasized about trying out for cheerleader the next year. The boys had finished their practice early. The girls were still cheering. We still had an hour before my mother was to pick us up. My brother and some of his friends came over to where I was. He told me one of his friends, that he knew I had a crush on, wanted to talk with me in the back dressing room and showers. He said I should go see what he wants. Then he volunteered to walk there with me. We walked into the dressing room. I said hello to the boy I liked and then noticed three other boys from the football team coming into the room. They held me down. One put a dirty sock in my mouth, and each one, including my brother, raped me. I was terrified. My brother had offered me up to them. I was humiliated and ashamed. My brother told me he'd kill me if I ever told anyone. I never told, back then.

"After a year, my brother began raping me regularly. He was big and very strong. I was glad he used condoms. The first six times, I was too terrified to tell. Then I finally told my mother, and nothing happened. She said not to tell anyone else. She was worried about him going to jail. I turned sixteen and moved out of the house. Momma didn't try to stop me. My house wasn't safe for me.

"If anything like this is happening to you, tell. Don't keep blaming yourself and being a victim. It's not your fault. Tell someone with the power to help you and to help get you out of the environment where it's happening."

The sheriff went to the microphone. "Thank you, Teresa, for sharing your experiences. From RAINN.org, 'Perpetrators of child sexual abuse are often related to the victim. Child victims often know the perpetrator. Among cases of child sexual abuse reported to law enforcement, out of the yearly 63,000 sexual abuse cases substantiated, or found to have strong evidence, by Child Protective Services (CPS):

- 80% of perpetrators were a parent
- 6% were other relatives
- 5% were "other" (from siblings to strangers)
- 4% were unmarried partners of a parent

❖❖❖

"Barbara Miller will be our next speaker," said Betty Jackson. "But first, Sheriff Raymer will present a couple of legal definitions."

Sheriff Raymer explained, "Alabama no longer separately codifies the offense of statutory rape, which some of you may have heard was the law concerning an older person having sex with a young person. Instead, what you think of as statutory rape, has been included in the following definitions from the Code of Alabama:

'Rape in the first degree: Sexual intercourse with a member of the opposite sex, where either:

- The offender uses forcible compulsion;
- The victim is incapable of consent by reason of being physically helpless or mentally incapacitated; or
- The offender is sixteen years of age or older and the victim is less than twelve years old.

'Rape in the second degree: Sexual intercourse with a member of the opposite sex where either:

- The offender is sixteen years old or older and the victim is between twelve and sixteen years old, provided that the victim is at least two years younger than the offender; or
- The victim is incapable of consent by reason of being mentally defective.'"

"Hello, I'm Barbara Miller. I was asked to tell you about my experiences. When I was fifteen years old, my mother drove me each morning, on her way to work, to the private Christian school I attended. I had girls' basketball practice after school each day. I was really good and a scout from a university had already talked with me and my parents about a scholarship.

"The friend I rode home with each day after practice had an accident and broke her leg. She mentioned to her cousin, we'll call him Steve, that I would be without a ride home. Steve worked at a grocery store in the city where I was going to school, lived in our rural community about ten miles from the city, and got off work each day about a half hour before my practice was over. He volunteered to give me a ride home each day. My parents knew his parents, met Steve, and finally said it would be okay.

"Steve was twenty-six at that time. You can't tell it now, but I was cute back then. Before long, Steve was flirting with me each day on the way home. Sometimes he brought us drinks and a snack of some kind from the store. Then, he said we should stop somewhere to leisurely finish our snack before going home. So, he pulled off the highway onto a field road and parked under a shady tree.

"We listened to the radio and talked. He flirted the whole time and told me I was beautiful. I was flattered by the attention, especially so because he was older and so handsome. He started holding my hand while we talked. Then he started kissing my hand. One day, he asked to kiss me, and I let him. He kept kissing me. I enjoyed the kissing. I was completely inexperienced and naïve. I hadn't ever had a date. My parents said I could start dating at sixteen.

"As the days went by, he began to fondle my breasts while we were kissing. He continually tried to go farther. I said no, but he persisted and kept inching closer and closer while we kissed. Then he stimulated my genitals with his hand. I still said no to sex. He wanted me to touch his privates. I was curious. I had never seen a grown man's penis before and wanted to see what it looked like. He pulled it out and told me I could make it grow large. He took my hands and had me rub his penis. He asked me to kiss it. He pushed me to oral sex for him and praised me for it. He told me he wanted to do the same for me and said I would like it and that all teenagers do it for each other. He continued pushing a little farther each day. One day, after I had rubbed his dick, I agreed that he could stimulate me orally. After a few minutes of that, he quickly moved up on top of me and before I realized what was happening, he was inside me.

We were having sex. Each day after that, he stopped and wanted sex. He kissed and petted and pushed me until I gave in. He never used a condom, and I got pregnant. We continued having sex on the way home from my school each day. He told me he loved me, and I believed him.

"I didn't tell my parents I was pregnant for four months. I didn't know how. I knew they would be angry. My father wanted to kill Steve and instead, was about to call the police to report him. I didn't want Steve to go to prison. Based on my age, fifteen, and him at twenty-six, he would be looking at a conviction of second degree rape and a sentence of between two and twenty years, and a fine. Of course, I didn't know at that time what the sentence could be. But I did know he would go to prison, and I didn't want my child's father to be in prison. I wanted to save my child from knowing his or her father was or had been in prison, and from ever having to tell that to anyone.

"I cried and begged my parents not to call the police until my father finally agreed not to call right then. Later, I would beg him again not to call. My mother took me to an obstetrician and before long, I had my daughter. At the hospital filling out paperwork, the staff realized my age and that I wasn't married. They reported it to the police. Again, I didn't want my daughter's father in prison. I had turned sixteen and would be able to marry if Momma and Daddy would sign their permission. They didn't want to.

"They didn't want me married to him. They told me all the reasons why I needed not to marry him. Momma also asked if I really loved him. I didn't immediately say yes, which she pointed out. I told her I did love him, even though I wasn't really sure. I enjoyed the intimate moments we'd had, and his flattery. I enjoyed feeling like I was grown up having sex, and I enjoyed the sex. Momma pointed out that I had never spent any time with him except on those rides home from school when he was trying to impress me and trying to have sex with me. She said I didn't know how he would act when he wasn't trying so hard, or when he was having a bad day, or when money was tight, or when the baby was crying all night keeping him awake. She begged me to let go of the notion of marrying him. I paid no attention to any of her logical reasons and begged them to let me marry him, so he wouldn't go to prison. In my fantasy, I expected us to live happily ever after. They finally agreed, and we were quickly married.

"Fast forward, and my mother was absolutely right. He still expected sex anytime he wanted it, but he stopped treating me special almost immediately. He didn't make enough money to take care of me and the baby and was always yelling about it. We argued. My parents helped me some. He got meaner and meaner with me as time went by and before long, he was hitting and punching me. I was so ashamed of the mess I had gotten myself into that I didn't tell anyone he was beating me or that if I said no to sex, he raped me.

"I finally told my parents everything, moved back in with them, and they helped me get a divorce. I got my GED and started community college. Meanwhile, this man who turned out to be so horrible had joint custody of my daughter. I don't think he loved her. He seemed to only want to use her to hurt me more. As she got older, she begged me to not make her go with him, and she said he was mean to her. It took several years to get the evidence needed to keep him from being alone with my daughter. Now he can only have supervised visitation with her, but he rarely bothers anymore. It was agony for me, my daughter, and my parents when he had joint custody.

"I'm telling you my embarrassing story so maybe you won't make my mistakes. Even though I was curious, I wasn't ready at fifteen to be having sex and was certainly not ready to get married at sixteen to a man eleven years older than me who had taken advantage of me and my innocence and curiosity. I beg of you to take your time, but if you do find yourself in a situation where you're being taken advantage of, or beaten, or raped, or abused in any way, please tell. Don't wait to do it. Tell right away. Shine the light on the situation."

Betty Jackson told the students the location of the Rape Crisis Center, about their services, and how to get in touch with them. She introduced her husband, Jerry.

"Hello, I'm Jerry Jackson. I worked for many years as a counselor and now I volunteer at the Center. Many believe rape is only about women. It's not. I'm going to talk about what no one wants to talk about. That's why we don't have a volunteer speaker here to tell his personal story, because very few men who have experienced rape or molestation want to talk about it. Fewer still want to speak about it in a group setting like this. Men think they're supposed to be tough guys and some think if they've been raped, it makes them not tough, and not a real man. That's not true, of course, but it's one of their many feelings. They also have some of the same feelings as women do after being raped- shame, embarrassment, and guilt about not being able to stop it from happening. Some feel vulnerable or depressed and may question whether they somehow did something to cause it. They are angry and may respond by acting out.

"You've already heard about the huge numbers of children, including young boys who are sexually abused. It may be by a male in the family, a neighbor, a coach, a teacher, a stranger, or even a priest or other leader in a church. These boys or teenagers carry the abuse with them the rest of their lives.

"There are those who are incarcerated who are raped. It's rampant in our prisons and disgraceful that it's being allowed to continue. Some in prison are pressured into joining groups or gangs who rape others. I counseled a man one time who was in such a group. He was in prison for a drug violation. He was afraid if he didn't join in with a group who raped others, he would become one of their victims. He got out of prison and continued his life. Later, a man who had been in prison in the group with him got out and found him. One day, they were riding together in a car. The man who had recently gotten out was driving. He saw a young, small-framed, male teenager walking down the road. The guy stopped and offered the boy a ride. The boy accepted. The driver drove to a secluded area, and the two men raped the boy and left him there.

"The man I counseled said he hadn't done anything like that since getting out of prison until the other man showed up. He didn't think he would have except for the presence of the ex-convict with whom he shared this previous behavior of raping vulnerable men. You need to know it happens.

"Male or female, something else that happens is that when your body is stimulated in its erogenous zones, it's wired to respond. Ideally, you're with someone you love when this stimulation happens. But, what if you're not? What if you're in a situation where you're being raped, or abused, or forced to participate against your will? What if you're terrified when it happens? And what if your body still responds to being stimulated and some of what is happening feels good, even though you're scared? If you're male, what if you get an erection while you're being raped or fondled, or for a male or female, what if you have an orgasm?

"People usually feel guilty if their bodies respond in these situations. They might think there's something wrong with them. It's just your body doing what's normal. It has nerve endings all over it, and they don't distinguish whether the stimulation is coming from someone you love and trust or from an abuser or rapist.

"If a male has been raped or abused by a man and experienced any pleasurable feeling during it, he might associate those pleasurable sexual feelings with that man or someone else who looks like the abuser. The victim might even become sexually aroused by thoughts of that man or seeing him or someone like him, and might at the same time be disgusted. This doesn't mean the person is gay or homosexual. It means those feelings were associated with the person who stimulated them.

"Rape or abuse isn't the fault of the victim. The person to blame is always the perpetrator. Confusing and complex feelings and emotions concerning these issues often get buried deep inside someone who has been victimized. Sometimes, a victim has emotions and behaviors in his or her life and cannot understand where they come from. If you or someone you know would like to talk, give us a call."

The sheriff took the microphone. "Out of the sexual abuse cases reported to Child Protective Services in 2013, 47,000 men and 5,000 women were the alleged perpetrators.

Sexual assault occurs:

- 55% at or near the victim's home
- 15% in an open public place
- 12% at or near a relative's home
- 10% in an enclosed but public area, such as a parking lot or garage
- 8% on school property

"As sheriff of Clayborne County, if you've been or if you ever are the victim of rape or sexual assault, I'm on your side. I'll do whatever I can to help you and to catch the person or people who hurt you. I'm here to tell you, Clayborne County has adopted a zero-tolerance policy for sexual assault and all sex crimes.

"I heard you all laugh about the word penis earlier. Well, boys, I'll give you a more common word and tell you straight up, in words you use, with no sugar coating: if you boys stick your dick in any hole that doesn't belong to you, without permission, I'm going to put you in prison. Or even with permission or encouragement, you better stay away from younger girls and young boys. There's a reason young girls are called jail bait. Leave them alone. Fall in love with someone your own age.

"If any of you want to know more about the different classifications and penalties for sexual crimes, see me after. There are categories we didn't talk about at all, like sodomy, sexual torture, and more. If you do like your momma taught you and keep your hands to yourself, you'll probably be all right.

"Domestic violence is a problem as well. There are brochures here on it. If you have issues with anger, if you feel the need to control the person you're dating or later are married to, or have feelings of inadequacy, please see a counselor to help you, so I never have to show up on your doorstep with handcuffs.

"I ask you to be kind to one another. Care about the people around you. You never know what someone else is going through. You don't know what's going on in his or her home when no one is looking, when the lights are out. You don't know what secrets your peers are keeping, what they are too ashamed and afraid to tell. You don't know who here has already been sexually assaulted or abused, or who is still being abused. Be kind to one another.

"Remember, the numbers say ages twelve to thirty-four are the highest risk years for crimes of sexual violence, and that females ages sixteen to nineteen are four times more likely than the general population to be victims of these crimes. If you see someone you believe may have been sexually assaulted or abused, reach out to them. You can make a difference, and you may be the only one who notices their pain, their behavioral changes, their suicidal talk.

"Be careful out there. There's safety in numbers. Go places with a group of friends and stay together, watch out for each other. Never leave a friend behind. Remember seven out of ten instances of sexual assault are committed by someone known to the victim. But it'll be less likely to happen to you if you have several friends with you, and you're watching out for each other. So, take care and call us if you need us.

"We thank you for your attention to today's speakers. Feel free to stay behind to talk with any of the speakers about anything, for yourself or for a friend."

Please note: Definitions and penalties for sex crimes vary from state to state. Please consult state and federal laws for the most up to date information.

CHAPTER 40

The Missing

*W*hen the roll is called up yonder, I'll be there..." sang the congregation of the Greatest Love Baptist Church. As they sat on the cushioned pews, the minister of music retreated, and Pastor Stevenson approached the pulpit for the announcements, remembrances, and the morning prayer. After his mention of the various prayer requests, he added, "Let's all pray for the families of the six missing men, our neighbors from across the river in Shorterville, Georgia."

Gabe put his arm around and gently squeezed his wife. He leaned to her and softly kissed her on the cheek, something he had never done in public before. Gayle smiled at him with love in her eyes.

Sheriff Raymer and Angelica sat a few rows behind them. Jack tensed with the pastor's mention of the missing men, and then wondered about Gabe's reaction. Did they suspect?

When Angelica felt his energy shift, she reached out for his left hand. His right arm rested on the back of the pew behind her with his hand around her right arm. He gave his left hand to her, and she sandwiched it between her hands, resting it in her lap and pulling him back from wherever he had gone. The pastor prayed, and Jack kissed her on the cheek. She opened her eyes, turned her head to him, and he kissed her on the lips. She smiled, closed her eyes, and bowed her head.

Senator Billy sat across the aisle, eyes wide open, looking frequently toward Sheriff Raymer.

After the service and the pastor's closing prayer was over, Jack stood from the prayer altar. The pastor spoke, shook his hand, and moved to the front door to speak to everyone as they departed. Billy pulled Jack to the side in the parking lot. "I need to talk with you before I leave for Montgomery tomorrow. Can you meet me at nine a.m. at the same place?" Billy asked.

"I'll see you there," Jack said.

Senator Billy closed the door behind him at his home to watch the evening news undisturbed. An earlier recording, which Billy hadn't seen, replayed. A reporter interviewed Police Chief Phil Ready of Shorterville, Georgia. He mentioned the six missing men of the area. He asked for the public's assistance, saying they had no leads in the disappearances.

"Jack, I didn't sleep at all last night. I tossed and turned and couldn't get this out of my head," Billy said.

"Maybe you should have taken something, Billy. What was on your mind?"

"You know what was on my mind. Those missing men the pastor mentioned at church yesterday. He didn't name them, but it was on the news last night. Those names, Jack. Those are the names of the rapists!"

"Really? How about that."

"Don't play with me, Jack; this is serious."

"I didn't see the news last night, Billy. I was spending time with Angelica, which was much more fun than watching the news, I'm sure. What did they say?"

Billy repeated everything to Jack.

"Jack, what have you done?" Billy asked.

"I don't know what you're talking about. I do about the same things every day. Things are slow paced around here, and I like it that way. That's why I chose to live here."

"Are you telling me you don't know anything about those missing men or how they went missing?" Senator Billy asked.

"That's exactly what I'm telling you. Why would I know anything about them? They live in Georgia. My jurisdiction stops at the river. I wouldn't be investigating Georgia missing persons cases."

"You know that's not what I'm asking, Jack. I remember what you swore you would do to them. Did you do it, Jack? Did you kill them? And why are they saying six men? There were seven men. Is there still one out there?"

"Wow, Billy. Are you wearing a wire or something? Take your clothes off and let's see. Got a wire here in your truck? Let's take a walk. Oh, on second thought, that's not necessary. I haven't done anything, Billy. Have you? Maybe you killed those men. Maybe those guys got scared, got on their motorcycles and all left town together without telling the police chief they were going. They don't strike me as being the type to report to anybody when they're leaving town, especially to the police chief. Why, they're probably partying in Miami, or Atlanta, or somewhere even as we speak."

"Okay, Jack. Okay. I get it. You're not going to talk about it. But I can tell you, I'm grateful they're missing, and I hope they're dead, and burning in hell. And anybody who did kill them deserves some angel wings. Well, maybe not angel wings, but I am certainly grateful. Getting rid of scum like that is just a huge public service."

"I know you did it," Billy went right back to it. "I don't know how. I can't even imagine how it could be done. I could never do it. I don't have the courage of a snail. Thank you, Jack, for doing it. I can walk down the street without being afraid. I can let my children play outside and feel less afraid for them. I can work in Montgomery and not worry as much for the safety of my wife. I owe you for doing it, Jack. Thank you." The senator had tears in his eyes. "But now, I'm worried about the seventh man." Red faced and trembling, Billy shook his head. One of the tears slid down his cheek. He wiped it away with a shaky hand and then held his head with both hands, covering his face.

"Billy, Billy. Look at me." Jack touched his arm, and Billy looked up.

"I heard the seventh man is with the other six."

"Really? Really, Jack? Oh, good. Thank God. That's good. Thank you, Jack."

"Billy, here, this is a phone number for you. Put it in your phone now, label it George or some other name, and hand me back the paper. That's to a burner phone I bought. I'm only going to check it once a day unless there's some reason to check it more often. If you need to meet with me or tell me something, call me on it, and I'll call you back with it. The ringer will be turned off, and it'll be hidden at my home. This will be just for now, until all this is over. There will still be times when we run into each other in town, which is fine. If you need me fast, you can still call the office or my regular cell. Just not too often. If there's no rush, call this number."

CHAPTER 41

Missing Person's Report

Sheriff, I reckon you saw on the news about those missing men across the river. There's an older woman that's come in and says her grandson is missing. He lives here in Clayborne County. Do you want me to give her to somebody else to take the report, or do you want to talk to her?" Sheila, the sheriff's assistant, asked.

"Go ahead and fill in the names and addresses and basic stuff on the report form in the computer, and then bring her to me. I'll pull the report up and add to it after I talk with her. Thank you, Sheila."

Patrice Robinson, called Patty, age seventy was brought to the sheriff's office.

The sheriff stood, shook her hand, and introduced himself. She was about five feet tall with gray hair, pulled back into a ponytail.

"Please have a seat, Mrs. Robinson," the sheriff said, noticing she was very thin.

"It's Miss. Just call me Patty. Everybody does."

"Would you like some coffee? I just made a fresh pot," the sheriff said.

"Yes, sir. Black, no sugar. Thanks." He handed it to her in a white styrofoam cup.

"So, your grandson is missing?" He set his jumbo mug on his desk beside a yellow legal pad where he was about to take notes.

"What's your grandson's name?"

"Douglas MacArthur Dinkins. We call him Dougie."

"When was the last time you saw your grandson?"

"It's been about three or four months ago. He doesn't come around much anymore." The sheriff jotted down notes.

"What makes you think he's missing, Miss Patty?"

"The house he lives in is rented. His landlord called me this morning, saying he hasn't paid and when he went over there, the place was a mess. He said it looked like he might have moved out, but he wasn't sure, so he called me. I'm listed as his emergency contact next of kin. I went over there, and it is a mess. He isn't Mr. Clean, but he normally keeps things tidy and straight. At least every time I've been there, it was that way."

"So, he paid his rent at the first of last month?"

"The landlord said he was paid through the end of last month but hasn't paid this month. He said the last time he saw Dougie was three months ago when he paid his rent for three months. He said Dougie, most of the time, pays for three or four months at a time. He said Dougie is never late with his rent and is one of the best renters he has because he normally only sees him three or four times a year."

"Do you know how much his rent is, Miss Patty?"

"I believe the landlord said it's $500 a month. He asked if I want to pay it this month, but I can't afford to pay his rent. I have bills of my own to pay."

"So, he pays $2,000 all at once on his rent?"

"That's what the man said."

"Where does Dougie work?"

"I don't know. I haven't heard anything about him having a job."

"Where does he get the money to pay his rent and other bills?"

"I don't know, Sheriff."

"Do you give him money?"

"I have from time to time, but it's been a long time, probably not in the last three years. He didn't always pay it back years ago, but he did the last few times he borrowed. I saw those other missing boys from Georgia on the news. There were two of 'em I recognized from the last time I went to Dougie's house. They were at his house."

"What were their names?"

"I don't know their names. I just noticed their faces and knew I'd seen 'em there at Dougie's."

"I'll let the Georgia authorities know. Dougie might be with those Georgia boys. So, the landlord said it looks like he's moved out. How did it look to you, Miss Patty?"

"Well, it looked like he could've moved out, but I just don't believe he would've without saying something to me."

"But, you said, he hardly visits you at all now and hasn't been to see you in the last four months or so."

"I reckon that's right. His truck was gone when I got over there, and his neighbor down the road said it hasn't been there in weeks. The door to the house stood wide open. The screen door was closed. Inside, it looked like somebody had gone through everything in the whole house. Things were strewn all over the floor. Everything that could be taken was gone. The television, stereo, the microwave, even his bed."

"So, he might have moved then?"

"I suppose he might have, but I just believe he would tell me if he was leaving, and the other thing, he would have taken all his clothes. There were too many of his clothes left there in the house."

"Miss Patty, did you touch things in the house or move things around?"

"No, sir, I was afraid to."

"I'm going to send a detective back there with you. He'll take pictures and dust for fingerprints and try to find other evidence there in the home. After he gets finished, you can take any of your grandson's things that you want, back to your house. I imagine the landlord will be cleaning the place out for the next renter and will put everything that's left there out by the side of the road for trash pickup."

"Yes, sir, that's what he said. He was nice about it though and said if I wanted him to, he'd send the people that usually cleans and puts everything out to the road, and they can help me pack things up. He even said he'd have them carry everything over to my house. I thought that was mighty nice of him."

"Miss Patty, where are Dougie's parents?"

"Dead, both of 'em. They were both involved with drugs and both died of it. His daddy got shot, probably ten years ago. My daughter was on those opioids and drank too. She was on meth and crack and some of all of it I think before it was over. She withered away and finally overdosed. I expect Dougie's mixed up in some of that mess too. It's a shame, it is. And ain't none of 'em here to take care of me." She shook her head.

"I've pulled up, here in the computer, the information on Dougie's truck, and I've put in a BOLO, or a Be on the Look Out, for the truck. I've entered Dougie's information here in the computer too and listed him as missing. I have this photo. Can you see my screen? It's from a few years back when he was arrested. Does he still look like this, or do you have a more recent photo of him?"

"That looks like him."

"Come with me, Miss Patty. I'm going to walk with you back up front. You'll wait there, and I'll get a detective to go with you to your grandson's house. Want some more coffee for the road?"

"Don't mind if I do. Thank you kindly, Sheriff."

"You're welcome, Miss Patty. Going forward, it'll be the detective who will be working with you. They'll give you a business card, in case you need to call them. You'll probably be getting a call from some of the Shorterville, Georgia detectives too.

"Dear God," the sheriff was back in his office. Elbows on his desk, his hands in front of his face, he said, "Dear God. I have taken that woman's only relative. She doesn't have anybody left to take care of her. What have I done?"

CHAPTER 42

Parents Have Rights

I'm so glad you came. I am bored out of my mind." Emma hugged her best friend, Hayden. "Sit on the couch, Hayden. This carpet has seen better days."

"Where's Maddie?" Hayden asked about Emma's dog.

"She's in the backyard getting some fresh air."

"You're not with her?"

"Momma doesn't want me anywhere that someone might see me, so I'm stuck here in this room, bored out of my gourd. What have you been up to? What do you have in that huge bag? Where did you get it?"

"It was a freebie I got when I ordered something online. I brought you your books from your locker, and I went around to all your teachers and got your assignments."

"What are you talking about? Momma said she took me out of school. How do I still have books in a locker and assignments?"

"I don't know. But I came across your locker combination in my planner and decided to look inside to see if you left anything. All your books and everything else was still there.

Here's your tampons and your sweater." Laughing, Hayden threw her the box of tampons and pulled the sweater from her bag.

"I wondered if your mother didn't officially withdraw you from school. I knew I couldn't ask in the office. I decided to ask the teachers for your assignments, and they gave them to me with no problems. They obviously haven't been told you've withdrawn. If you were withdrawn, they would know and would have to take your name off their roster. They asked, and I told them I didn't know when you'd be back, but I didn't want you to be behind. That seemed to do it for them. So maybe you can take and pass your finals and do all your homework and still pass your senior year. It's worth a try, don't you think?"

"Amazing, Hayden. You're amazing. Thank you. And I'm so bored, I actually want to do the homework. I suppose after I miss a certain number of days, that might automatically kick me out. I don't know the rules because I rarely miss days."

Hayden stacked all the books and a folder full of assignments and instructions on the coffee table in front of the couch. "I'll take in your completed homework and keep bringing your new assignments."

Hayden smiled. "I also brought you a present from the outside world," she said. She reached into her bag and pulled out a box. "Since you can't go out for contraband, ta-da, a dozen donuts of all varieties!"

"Oh, my goodness! Let's eat one now," Emma said. "I guess it's being pregnant... I'm hungry all the time. I mean really, all the time. Momma sends over a plate of food by Noah for each meal. But Noah has been so good to me. He brings me snacks. He brought me a huge bag of chips the other day and a package of chocolate chip cookies. They were divine. He brings healthy stuff too, carrots and apples, but he gets a hug when he brings ice cream and junk food. I don't know why I want that stuff so much. You know I've always eaten a lot of fruits and veggies."

"Then I'm glad I decided on donuts instead of grapes. Your body's just going through a lot right now."

"Umm, grapes sound good too." They both laughed.

"Have you looked up on the internet information about being pregnant, so you know what to expect?"

"Momma confiscated my laptop right after the phone."

"Oh, Emma, why?"

"She's trying to cut me off from the outside and from email."

"Well, you have the phone I brought to you. I've been wondering why you haven't called or emailed or even sent a text. I've got the number but was afraid to call because if your mother was here with you, she might hear the phone ringing, the one you're not supposed to have."

"Hayden, you brought it and then we visited, and you left. We forgot that those phones have to be activated using another phone."

"Crap. Let's do it now. Go get it. Couldn't you use Noah's phone to set it up?"

"I didn't want to get him in trouble again. I've gotten him into a lot lately. I was planning to do it Sunday with the house landline phone, while they were at church, but I forgot all about it."

"Are you not even seeing your parents, Emma?"

"Not a lot. Maybe it's best for now. I don't know. I did have supper with them one night. Noah wanted me there for some news." Emma told her about the article Noah brought home and the fight they had at supper. She showed her the printout of the article.

"Emma, have you not seen any news? This has been on the news every day for about a week now. So, are you saying these are the men who raped you?"

"Those are six of the seven," Emma said and then told her Noah's theory that the sheriff might have made them disappear. "You have to swear you won't repeat that to anyone, not a single soul. Those guys could have just gotten scared because the sheriff figured out who they are, and they could have just left town for a while."

"Okay, I swear. Wow, this is wild stuff, Emma."

"Daddy was so great about sticking up for me and the sheriff." Emma told her the details.

"I know it'd be a relief to you to believe they're dead. If they are alive, I hope the sheriff puts them in prison for a long, long time. I've done some looking around on the internet, Emma, and I have to show you something I read about, but you're not going to like it."

"What?"

Hayden got out her laptop from her bag. "What's your Wi-Fi password?" She started typing. "Emma, this says that even if a woman is raped, it doesn't negate the rights of the father as a parent, and he will still have visitation rights."

"What? No way. That can't be true," Emma said.

"I know. It's awful, right? I've got it now. Here, listen to this, 'Without any legislation stopping a sexual assailant from claiming parental rights of a child, individuals are free and clear to pursue custody or visitation rights of their biological offspring.'"

"That can't be right. A rapist wouldn't have the right to visit. That would be like living in an ongoing domestic terrorist horror movie. What site are you looking at?"

"It's from CNN Health. It's for real, Emma. Listen to this, 'Seven states don't have any laws preventing a rapist from claiming parental rights, but that's not to say that these states are oblivious to the issue. Maryland, for one, has been working for years to pass a law that would allow a rape victim to terminate her attacker's parental rights.

'Forty-three other states and the District of Columbia have legislation that offers at least some protection to prevent rape victims from facing their attackers over parental rights; eight of those laws were adopted in 2016.

'But these legislative protections vary greatly. In twenty states and D.C., a rape conviction is required before a victim can request termination of parental rights.

'For advocates, this is a problematic barrier, since the majority of sexual assaults don't even make it to prosecution, according to the Bureau of Justice Statistics. Between 2005 and 2010, just 36% of the nearly 300,000 annual average rape or sexual assault victimizations were reported to police, the bureau reports. Even when you look at both reported and unreported rapes during that time period, roughly 12% of victimizations resulted in arrests.

'That means in nearly half the states that have legislation meant to prevent rapists from claiming parental rights, a victim is still vulnerable to having to face her attacker if there wasn't a conviction in her case, and that's if she reported it and if it was prosecuted.'"

"Oh my God! That's horrifying. I already don't want to have the baby of one of those scum bags, but if I do, there's no way I could share custody with one of them and see him every other week, and I especially couldn't let any of those men walk away with my child."

"It's unbelievable," Hayden said.

"What about our state? Does it have information on all the individual states?"

"Let me look."

"Maybe we've got protections here," Emma said.

"It says, 'Alabama is one of the few states that doesn't have any law to prevent rapists from seeking custody of children conceived during an attack.' Oh, Emma, I'm so sorry. How awful."

Emma picked up her bed pillow she had been using on the couch. She hugged it tightly up to her chest and cheek, and lay over onto the back of the couch, crying.

"I shouldn't have told you. I shouldn't have read all this to you, Emma. I'm so sorry," Hayden said, trying to put her arm around Emma.

"It's not your fault, Hayden. You just let me know how it is. Hayden, would you help me?"

"If I can, Emma. Help you with what?"

"Help me abort this fetus."

"Oh my God, Emma. I'll drive you to have it done, but I… I… just can't do it myself. What if I hurt you? I can't. I'd have no idea what to do."

"I see."

"Emma, I'm sorry. It's getting late. I've got to go home now."

"Go."

Hayden left, and Emma continued crying into her pillow.

CHAPTER 43

Fingerprints

S tanding on the cement front porch of a little white house, the sheriff knocked on the door. Patty Robinson opened the front door.

"Good morning, Miss Patty. I want to talk with you a few minutes. Could we sit here on your porch?"

"Morning, Sheriff."

"Your flowers are beautiful. I noticed a hummingbird here a minute ago."

"I have seen six hummingbirds here at the same time. They say, 'no news is good news.' I don't imagine this to be good news. Have a seat."

The sheriff eased into a rocking chair, still admiring the flowers growing around the porch. "Your sunflowers sure are pretty. Every time I plant sunflowers, I come back around later in the day and find tiny little holes where the squirrels have dug up every single seed I planted and eaten it."

"After you plant the sunflower seeds, water them well,

and then sprinkle cayenne pepper all over the top of the soil. The squirrels will leave 'em be," said Miss Patty. "If it rains, put out more cayenne."

"That's a great idea. I don't know why I didn't think of it. Miss Patty, there is a press conference scheduled for later this morning, and I wanted to update you before then and tell you what we've learned."

Patty Robinson looked up at him, staring.

"You mentioned you saw two of the missing Georgia men at your grandson's house."

"Yes, sir."

"You know the detectives dusted your grandson's house for fingerprints. The fingerprints of all six of the missing Georgia men were found in your grandson's place. We shared everything we found with the authorities in Georgia working on the six missing men cases because we know your grandson knows those men and they have been in his home."

"Yes, sir. That makes sense."

"Your grandson's truck was found in Miami, Florida. The truck was being driven by a man with a large quantity of drugs hidden in a secret compartment of the truck. It appears the truck may have been used to traffic drugs. There was no sign of your grandson or any of the others. Right now, the disappearances of all seven men are suspected to be drug-related disappearances."

"I understand."

"Would you like to say anything at the press conference today, Miss Patty?" If you want to make an appeal to or on behalf of your grandson, I can get you on the agenda."

"No, sir. There's no point. If he's alive, he knows where I am. I don't expect anybody's holding him for ransom, or against his will. There's no point in me being there at all."

"I thought I'd give you the choice. There's one other thing. Right now, your grandson's truck has been impounded. They'll go all over it, looking for evidence. If the truck itself isn't considered evidence, they'll eventually let it go. It might take a long while. I've listed you as the only living relative of your grandson. So, in the absence of your grandson, it may eventually come back to you. Along with the drugs found in the truck, there was a lot of money. It probably will all be seen as related to the buying and selling of illegal drugs. But I told them you had loaned your grandson some money and if there is any of the money not tied to the illegal drugs, it belongs to you. I doubt it will ever happen, but I thought I'd let you know just in case they ask. Remember to tell them you loaned him money to pay his rent, or for food, or whatever."

"Thank you, Sheriff. That's good of you. I know you didn't have to do that. I appreciate your effort. What's this?" She opened a white plastic bag on the table by the door. "There's an apple pie in here. Did you bring this?"

"Yes, ma'am. I was at the diner this morning and thought of you when I saw it."

"Thank you, Sheriff. Nobody's brought me anything like this since my husband died twenty years ago," she said. She reached out and hugged him. "I'll enjoy this."

"Well, I'll be going. If you have any questions, you know how to call us. I hope you have a good afternoon." She walked with him to his car. The wind moved something on her roof.

"What is that moving up there with the wind?" asked the sheriff.

"That storm the other day blew it loose," Miss Patty said. "I haven't had the money to call anybody to see to it."

"It looks like it just needs nailing back down," said the

sheriff. "But it needs doing before it gets any worse. That won't be a hard fix. I've got to go back to the office now, but I'll come back this afternoon after work and tack that down for you. I'll have to get a ladder and some supplies, and then I'll come take care of it."

"I don't know what to say. You're doing things no one has ever done for me. I've had to pay for everything all my life. Thank you so much. You're a good man, Sheriff."

"Sheila," the sheriff called to his assistant. "Would you please call Senator Billy and see if he wants to be here and say anything at the press conference later today? I imagine he will. I've never known him to pass up the chance to be on TV."

Police Chief Phil Ready, Sheriff Raymer, and Senator Billy all read statements for the press conference regarding the six missing men from Georgia and one from Alabama: Douglas MacArthur Dinkins, (aka Dougie Dinkins) of Alabama, and of Georgia: Carl Mitchell, Bert Taylor, Vince Kelley, Ned Collins, Oliver Banner, Paul Malcomb.

Chief Ready thanked Sheriff Raymer whose shared information cracked the case open, providing invaluable information. He reported Douglas Dinkins' truck was found in Miami, being used in drug trafficking; the disappearances of the men are all suspected of being drug related; no bodies have been found; the men remain missing.

CHAPTER 44

Choices Made

The sheriff's office received a call from the home of Gabe and Gayle Symner. An ambulance was dispatched to the home for Emma. Her parents and brother had been out of town for a long weekend at the beach. Emma didn't go. They returned home, and Noah found Emma on the floor of her room in the garage apartment when he went to take her a seashell and chocolate-covered peanuts.

Sheriff Raymer heard the dispatcher ordering the ambulance. Alarmed, he rerouted to the Symner home and arrived before the ambulance and emergency medical technicians. He grabbed his Trauma Combat Medical kit and ran to the door.

Noah was waiting. "It's Emma!" Noah yelled. "Follow me. This way." Noah led him, running to the upstairs garage apartment.

Inside the door of Emma's bedroom, the sheriff paused only for a moment, shocked at what he saw. Emma was lying on the floor beside her bed, naked from the waist down. There was a large puddle of blood. A straightened clothes hanger protruded from her body, with the other end still inside her vagina.

The sheriff hurried to her. His years in the Marines on the battle field kicked in and the tender feelings he had for Emma were, in an instant, stowed away to allow what must be done. He felt the carotid artery in her neck, checking for a pulse. It was faint.

"Gayle, get two folded top sheets, king size if you've got them. If not, bring what you've got," Sheriff Raymer ordered.

"Gabe, Noah, give me your belts." He removed the clothes hanger from her body.

"Help me," he told Gabe and Noah. "We need to elevate her pelvic area." He placed two pillows on the floor, put the two belts on top of them just as Gayle entered the room, carrying the sheets. Gabe, Noah, and the sheriff positioned Emma on top of the pillows. The sheriff took the sheets.

"Gayle, call the emergency room at the hospital. Tell them Emma's coming in and needs blood and emergency surgery. Tell them she's bleeding to death." Gayle stood in shock. "Gayle!" Sheriff Raymer yelled, "Go, call them now!"

"Noah, open these two rolls of gauze, but don't touch the gauze." Sheriff Raymer reached back and put on gloves from his emergency kit. On his knees in the blood, he parted Emma's legs and packed both rolls of gauze into her vagina. He positioned the heavy folded sheets on top of her lower abdomen and pelvic areas and tightened the belts as tight as he could get them, making a new hole in Gabe's belt.

"Noah, lean over her. Lay your arms on top of the sheets and keep steady pressure on her. We've got to stop the bleeding." Noah, on his knees, in his sister's blood, did as he was instructed.

The sheriff heard sirens in the distance. "Gabe, make sure Gayle called the ER and then go outside to wait for the ambulance. Tell them I said she is going straight to the ER and to bring in the stretcher when they come, so they don't have to go back after it. They can start the IV in the ambulance. She's got to get to the hospital right away. Gabe… tell them loudly." Gabe hurried out of the room.

The sheriff leaned down to check Emma's pulse again. He could barely detect it. Emma's eyes fluttered open. "Get them, Sheriff." Her voice was a whisper.

He dropped onto his elbow beside Emma's face and laying in her blood, he said,

"Emma, I did." He whispered in her ear, "Emma, I killed them all. You don't have to be afraid of them anymore. They're all dead. You hang on, Emma. Fight! Live, Emma!"

"I'm glad you killed them. Thank you, Sheriff," Emma said.

Noah smiled for a moment through his tears and then dropped his head, letting his forehead rest on the sheet between his arms as he wept.

The EMTs rushed into the room with the stretcher, followed by Gayle and Gabe. Emma's eyes fluttered shut. One of the EMTs pulled out his stethoscope to listen for her heartbeat.

"There's no pulse, she's gone," he said. "She's bled out."

"We're going to the hospital," Sheriff Raymer said.

"She's gone, Sheriff. You want to listen with the stethoscope?"

"No! Get up, we're going to the hospital now!" The sheriff and Noah lifted her onto the stretcher.

"We're going to the hospital. Get your ass in gear, man!" the sheriff ordered. He and Noah, covered in blood, got in the ambulance together with the technician. The sheriff administered CPR.

"Noah, keep pressure on her pelvis." Noah pressed down with his forearms as he had at the house. Tears streamed down his face.

"Emma, please don't die. Emma, please stay with me," he repeated.

Sheriff Raymer ordered the driver to radio the hospital and again asked them to be prepared. The IV was started. The sheriff continued CPR. The EMT administered artificial respiration using an Ambu bag.

The EMT talked of possible brain damage if Emma did come back. The sheriff nodded his head toward Noah, and told the EMT, "That's enough," wanting the EMT to curtail talk of brain damage in front of Noah.

"Emma, please don't die. Emma, please stay with me," Noah repeated.

CHAPTER 45

The Tie That Binds

Angelica held Sheriff Raymer's hand as they walked into the Greatest Love Baptist Church for the Sunday morning service. She was impressed Jack had attended church with her every Sunday since they started dating. It was important to her.

This morning, they didn't arrive as early as they normally did, allowing no chitchat time with others. The service would soon begin. Someone saw them coming in and nudged another who looked back. Someone else looked. In a matter of seconds everyone in the church had turned to watch them walk down the aisle to their usual seat. Complete silence, until sweet Mrs. Jacobs saw what was happening and suddenly began, *Blest Be the Tie That Binds,* on the organ. Angelica squeezed his hand and they glanced at one another.

Last evening, Jack had called her. Angelica knew he was upset and told him she would be right over. She wanted to be prepared and packed the things needed for this morning in an overnight bag, which was left in his living room.

When Angelica arrived, Jack told her about his evening with Emma. She hugged him and listened to all he felt he could tell her about Emma. Later, she fixed them hot soup, iced tea, and made cornbread to go with it. Afterwards, they rested on his bed. She cradled his head in the crook of her arm as though he were a baby. She kissed his forehead, rubbed her hand soothingly across his face, and sang to him until he slept.

When the morning came, Jack opened his eyes and found Angelica in his bed in a silky, cobalt-blue nightgown. He could hardly believe it, thinking at first it must be a dream. Her head was on his arm, and her arm was wrapped around his body. Her breasts were pressed against the side of his chest. He remembered the night before but quickly swept it away in favor of this marvelous new turn of fortune. Her eyes fluttered open.

"Good morning," she said.

"An excellent morning so far," he said. "I thought I was dreaming."

Angelica eased up onto her right elbow and kissed him. She kissed him again, letting her left hand move over his body.

"If you're trying to seduce me, it's working," he said and smiled.

"Good," she said. "Then I'll have my way with you."

Now they were seated, and the minister of music led the congregation in the singing of hymns. The choir sang specially prepared music, then the pastor delivered his message and ended it with a prayer. The invitational hymn was sung for the altar call. Sheriff Raymer had gone to the altar to pray every Sunday since he began attending with Angelica. Emma was still on his mind and in his heart. He looked into Angelica's eyes. She squeezed his hand.

"It's okay, mi amor, my love. Go if you want. It's okay," Angelica said.

He already had tears in his eyes. He turned, walked to the front, and knelt on the provided cushion. His hands were clasped together in front of him. He began to pray. The pastor noticed his tears and went to him, praying with him. Jack's shoulders moved up and down as he cried. He cried for Emma, for himself, for all the people he had killed over the last twenty-five years and the families who loved them, and he cried because Angelica seemed to love him, and he didn't feel worthy of her love, or God's love. He cried for all the many secrets in his life, and he prayed to keep his combat box locked and put away forever.

An elderly grandmother noticed and walked to the front of the church. She went to him, laid her left hand on his shoulder, raised her right hand toward heaven and said in an unexpectedly loud voice, "I'm praying for you, Sheriff. Praise God, help our sheriff."

Another came to him. "I'm praying for you, Sheriff. God hold you in His hands."

A procession of women came to him, laying hands on his back and shoulders, all affirming their prayers for him. They stood at the front of the church, raising a hand and saying, "Praise Jesus!" "Yes, Lord," and "Hallelujah!" The church hummed with their words and buzzed with movement in ways seldom heard or seen in a Baptist church.

They had all heard about Emma and how the sheriff had fought to save her.

The sheriff was overcome with what was going on inside him and the tremendous concern and support for him from the congregation. He wept, and finally, trying to get up, fell forward onto the floor, still crying.

Senator Billy had been watching. Tears streamed down

his face. With Jack's fall, Billy rushed to him. Angelica saw but made herself stay where she was. Senator Billy sat on the floor, gathered Jack into his arms, and hugged him. They both cried, rocking to and fro.

Slowly, the people returned to their seats. Billy and the pastor lifted Jack onto the front pew where Billy continued to hold him.

The pastor returned to the pulpit and the organist stopped at the end of the chorus she was playing.

"I'd like to say a special prayer for the Symner family, for Sheriff Raymer, Senator Billy, for all the friends and family of the Symners. Please remember them all in your prayers this week. I have never witnessed in this church such an outpouring of love and concern in the time I've been here. I am privileged and grateful just to have witnessed it. Thank you all." The pastor prayed the closing prayer and made his way to the front of the church as the people departed. Billy and Angelica walked with Jack out the side door to her car. Billy held Jack who was still crying.

"Jack, everything's going to be all right. It's going to work out," Billy said.

Angelica drove them back to Sheriff Raymer's home. She undressed him and put him to bed. She got him a single shot of tequila.

"This will help you feel better, mi amor," she said. She gave him ice water and bathed his face with a cold wash-cloth. Then she got in bed beside him. Again, she held him until he was asleep. Later, she put food in his oven to cook, set a timer, and rejoined him. She stayed with him the rest of the day.

CHAPTER 46

Senator Billy Wants Change

Senator Billy's publicist called a press conference at one p.m. and invited media from all over the state. She notified national network press concerning the subject and content of the senator's expected statements, knowing they might ask local affiliates for the video if it was of interest to them. Senator Billy contacted Betty and Jerry from the local Rape Crisis Center and asked them to invite any interested individuals to the press conference. He also asked Sheriff Raymer to attend.

Senator Billy stood at a podium positioned at the top of the steps leading into an abandoned brick building. Tall and lanky, and neatly groomed, he adjusted his tie, took off his sunglasses, and squinted from the brightness of the day.

Sheriff Raymer shook his hand. "Thank you, Billy, for yesterday."

"Think nothing of it, Jack. You would've done the same."

"Do I need to be afraid of what might come out of your mouth here today?"

"Nah, it'll be all right, Jack. I'm just going to say a few things that need to be said. Things that should have been said a long time ago. Things that need to come out of the closet and into this bright sunlight."

"Damn, Billy. I'm a tough guy, or at least I used to be, but you sure make me nervous about all this stuff."

"Look at the people. Betty and Jerry must have called the whole town," Billy said. "Look at the cars. They're still driving into the parking lot."

"Just as I was leaving to come, it was announced on TV," Jack said.

"Really? On what?"

"Well, the noon news, before the weather, and the Gene Regan Farm report."

"Probably the whole town was watching then."

"Good luck, Billy." Jack returned to his seat.

Billy checked his microphone. The power was turned off in the abandoned building. They brought a battery to operate the PA system. It worked.

"Good afternoon, ladies and gentlemen. Thank you for coming here today. I guess you're wondering why we are meeting here, outside of the city, in front of this abandoned building. Some of you may remember what this building used to be. It was a government building, a state crime lab.

"When there are budget shortfalls, if taxes aren't raised, there are cuts. Priorities have to be decided, like how much is cut from which state departments. What services, programs, prisons, roads, and bridges lose how much from their budgets.

"Money was cut from the budget of the Department of Forensic Sciences a good while back. This crime lab was closed, and staff was reduced across the state. This has contributed to a backlog across the state in prosecuting all types of criminal cases.

"I didn't know until recently that there is a tremendous backlog in the processing of rape kits. These are the kits used to collect forensic evidence when someone goes to the hospital after having been raped. I learned that thousands upon thousands of rape kits in our state have gone unprocessed and are sitting on shelves in evidence rooms.

"Many times, the DNA evidence is the strongest evidence in the prosecution of a rapist. Without this evidence, prosecutors often don't take the case to court. There are times when the DNA is what identifies the rapist, and without it, the rapist isn't arrested. In both scenarios, the victim has no closure.

"Mobile, Alabama has received two grants for processing their backlog of rape kits. Birmingham received one grant. In Mobile, an eighty-one-year-old woman went to court and testified against the man who raped her twenty-four years earlier. He was someone she didn't know, who kicked in her back door in the middle of the night and raped her. One of the grants provided the funding to process her rape kit, which led to his arrest and conviction, and finally, closure for this eighty-one-year-old grandmother.

"I want to tell you first, the people here in my home county, I've been working on legislation concerning several issues associated with the crime of rape, the first of which is to require the processing of rape kits. Somehow, the prosecution of rape and sexual assault seems to have been downgraded in priority. When state money is tight, we know certain things take priority, like murder cases. We know we must have strong roads and bridges, but processing of rape kits has been pushed back as a priority, it seems, behind almost everything, to the point of thousands not being processed, and an eighty-one-year-old woman waiting twenty-four years before hers was processed.

"I am asking, why have our legislators of the past put such

a low priority on testing the DNA evidence when a rape occurs? Do they not care about women? Maybe they don't know that men are also victims of sexual assault. Perhaps they are like me. I only recently learned about this staggering backlog of unprocessed rape kits.

"I am asking, why has our judicial system put such a low priority on prosecuting rapists? In doing this, they ignore the victimization of our daughters, wives, sons, mothers, and even grandmothers. What if it was your daughter? What if it was you?

"I am asking, why have our Alabama legislators not taken the time, or seen the importance of creating a pathway to deny parental rights to convicted rapists when the child is the product of his rape? We're one of only seven states in the United States who hasn't addressed this issue. Do you really want your daughter forced to see her rapist every other week when he takes her child and your grandchild for the weekend?

"Men in prison are raped. No one wants to talk about it. Some say, 'They're in prison, they deserve it.' But I ask, what if it was your son? What if your nineteen-year-old had too much to drink at a frat party during his first month of college, got behind the wheel, hit someone, killed them, and got fifteen years for manslaughter, with a side of daily gang rape. What does that do to a man for the rest of his life? Do you approve of this? Why is it allowed to continue?

"I am a supporter of the *Me Too* movement. But in light of the thousands of young boys who have been molested by church leaders, the ones molested by their coaches, their scout leaders, their family members, and men raped in prison and many other places, I say, *Us Too!* Sexual assault isn't just a crime against women. Remember, it happens to us too!

"If a male legislator has never raped anyone and honestly believes rape to be an abhorrent crime, why would he not create and pass laws on behalf of our daughters, our wives, our mothers, our grandmothers, our sons, and even our brothers; on behalf of all sexual assault victims?

"Ladies and gentlemen, if your legislators will not vote for these changes, then why would you vote to reelect them to represent you? Everyone at every level must take responsibility for what's happening now and insist that changes be made for the future.

"A veteran recently told me he was sent to a foreign country by us, the citizens of the USA. He said he was sent to kill people and that's what he did, even though, personally, he didn't have anything against the young men he killed. He was told they were the enemy, and it was all right to kill because it's war. He told me, when he got home, if he killed the man who raped his twelve-year-old daughter while he was in Afghanistan, he would go to prison for the rest of his life or sit on death row. He said the only difference is that the people and government of our county had declared war in one situation, but not the other. He was confused, and I am too.

"I say, *Declare War on Sexual Assault* and those who commit these traumatic and life-changing crimes! I say demand of your legislators, the kind of justice that is every citizen's right. Everyone deserves equal justice and laws that punish abusers and protect their victims. Thank you all, for coming today."

The people of River Rock and Clayborne county gave the senator a standing ovation. Later that night, the local news stations carried Billy's speech. National news networks picked up the story and parts of it were shown nationally.

CHAPTER 47

An Invitation

It was Saturday morning, and Jack Raymer was eating breakfast at home.

"Want another pancake, honey?" Angelica asked as she slid one onto Jack's plate.

"These are marvelous. I don't know how yours always turn out so great. Why don't mine ever taste like these?"

"It's the love I put in them, mi amor! Oh, I hear the mailman outside. I'll get it."

"We got a lot of mail today," Angelica said.

"Mommy, I'm hungry," five-year-old Maria said as she walked in, still wearing her pajamas.

"Here you go, my love, pancakes and bacon. I'll cut it up for you."

"More syrup, Mommy, please."

"Come on and eat, Maria, Daddy's taking you to the birthday party today while I buy groceries. You still have to get dressed and I will help you wrap your gift."

"Are you excited about the party, sweetheart?" Jack asked.

"It'll be fun, I think," Maria said.

"Here, Jack, this envelope is hand-written for you," said Angelica.

"Oh my God," Jack said after he opened it.

"Oh my God," Maria repeated.

"See, I told you not to say that in front of her. She's repeating everything. Maria, Daddy meant to say, Oh my goodness. Didn't you, Daddy?" She raised her eyebrows at him.

"Yes, darling. I meant, Oh, my goodness, and if I forget again, you remind me. Okay, Maria?"

"Okay, Daddy. I will."

"So, what I'm trying to tell you is, this is a graduation invitation from Emma. We are going to the University of Alabama for graduation. Here, let's see what she wrote. She says she's sorry it's been so long since she's seen us or written to us, but she thinks of us often. She says, 'Congratulations on winning another term in office. And when you see him, please tell Governor Billy I'm proud he won his election and thank him for me for all the work he's done to make things better for daughters, wives, mothers, and all women and men affected by sexual assault. He's made a good difference with his legislation.

"'You have to come to graduation. After all, I wouldn't be here if not for you. Let me know, and we can get together while you're here. You've got my number. Love Always and Forever, Emma.

P.S. You can stop sending money now!'"

~ The End ~

INFORMATION AND RESOURCES (USA)

Sexual Assault Links

RAINN (Rape, Abuse, Incest National Network)
1-800-656-HOPE (4673) – https://www.rainn.org y rainn.org/es

RAINN'S MISSION - RAINN is the nation's largest anti sexual violence organization. RAINN created and operates the National Sexual Assault Hotline in partnership with more than 1,000 local sexual assault service providers across the country and operates the DoD Safe Helpline for the Department of Defense. RAINN also carries out programs to prevent sexual violence, help survivors, and ensure that perpetrators are brought to justice.

End the Backlog - http://www.endthebacklog.org/
Men Can Stop Rape - www.mencanstoprape.org
National Sexual Violence Resource Center –
https://www.nsvrc.org - 717-728-9740
Alabama Coalition Against Rape - www.acar.org

Domestic Violence Links

CDC: Violence Prevention -
https://www.cdc.gov/violenceprevention/
Corporate Alliance to End Partner Violence -
https://nomore.org/why-the-corporate-alliance-to-end-partner-violence-capev-is-part-of-the-no-more-project/

Duluth Blueprint for Safety - https://www.theduluthmodel.org/duluth-blueprint-safety/
Futures Without Violence - https://www.futureswithoutviolence.org/
Men Against Violence - www.mavaw.org
Men Stopping Violence - www.menstoppingviolence.org
National Center on Domestic and Sexual Violence - www.ncdsv.org
National Child Abuse Hotline - www.childhelpusa.org
National Coalition Against Domestic Violence - www.ncadv.org
National Domestic Violence Hotline - www.ndvh.org
National Network to End Domestic Violence - www.nnedv.org
Office on Violence Against Women (OVW) - https://www.justice.gov/ovw - 202-307-6026
Partnership Against Domestic Violence - www.padv.org

Other Links

National Center for Victims of Crime - www.victimconnect.org - 1–855–4–VICTIM - 1-855-484 2846
National HIV/AIDS Hotline - 1-800-CDC-INFO - 1-800-232-4636
National Organization for Victim Assistance - www.trynova.org - 1-800-TRY-NOVA - 1-800-879-6682
Office for Victims of Crime - https://www.ovc.gov/welcome.html
Online Resource Directory of Crime Victim Services - https://ovc.ncjrs.gov/findvictimservices/

Alabama Information and Resources

- Alabama Coalition Against Rape / P.O. Box 4091 / Montgomery, AL 36104 - 334-264-0123 - www.acar.org
- Alabama Coalition Against Domestic Violence - www.acadv.org
- Alabama Crime Victims Compensation Commission / P.O. Box 231267 Montgomery, AL 36123-1267 - 334-290-4420 - www.acvcc.alabama.gov
- Alabama Attorney General's Office for Victims Assistance / Alabama State House / 11 South Union St. 3rd Floor / Montgomery AL 36130 - 334-242-7300 - 1-800-626-7676 - www.ago.state.al.us
- Governor's Office for Victims of Crime / State Capital / 600 Dexter Avenue / Montgomery, AL 36104 - 334-242-7100 www.ovc.ncjrs.gov/ResourceByState.aspx?state=al #tabs2
- House of Ruth Southeast Alabama –
- https://www.houseofruthdothan.org/ 334-793-5214 – Crisis Line – 800-650-6522 or 334-793-2232

❖❖❖

Signs of a Battering Personality

Many are interested in ways to identify if they're becoming involved with someone who will be physically abusive. Below is a list of behaviors seen in people who beat their partner; the last four signs listed are battering, but many women don't realize this is the beginning of physical abuse. The person who displays three or more of the other behaviors has a strong potential for physical violence- the more signs the person has, the more likely the person is a batterer. In some cases, a batterer may have only a couple of behaviors but they're exaggerated, like extreme jealousy. The abuser can be male or female.

1. JEALOUSY

At the beginning of a relationship, an abuser will always say that jealousy is a sign of love; jealousy has nothing to do with love. It's a sign of possessiveness and lack of trust. He will question the woman about whom she spends time with - family, friends, or children. As the behavior intensifies, he may call her frequently during the day or drop by unexpectedly. He may refuse to let her work for fear she'll meet someone else, or exhibit unusual behaviors such as checking her vehicle mileage and asking friends to watch her.

2. CONTROLLING BEHAVIOR

At first, the batterer will say this behavior is because he's concerned for the woman's safety, her need to use her time well, or her need to make good decisions. He will be angry if the woman is "late" coming back from the store or an appointment. He will question her closely about where she went, and to whom she spoke. As this behavior intensifies, he may not let the woman make personal decisions about the house, her clothing, or going to church. Also, he may withhold money from her and require that she ask his permission to leave the house or room.

3. QUICK INVOLVEMENT

Many battered women have dated or known their abuser for

less than six months before they were married, engaged, or living together. The relationship may start like a whirlwind and he may make passionate declaration such as, "You're the only person I've ever been able to talk to," or "I've never felt loved like this by anyone." He will pressure her for commitment to the relationship in such a way that the victim may feel guilty or that she is letting him down by wanting to slow down or break off the relationship.

4. UNREALISTIC EXPECTATIONS

Abusive people expect their partners to meet all their needs; they expect the partner to be the perfect spouse, parent, lover, and friend. They may say things like "If you love me, I'm all you need and you're all I need."

5. ISOLATION

The abusive person tries to cut the person off from all resources. If, for instance, the abusive person is a male and his partner has male friends, he might say she's a "whore" and if she has female friends, she's a "lesbian." The abusive person may accuse people who are supportive of the partner of "causing trouble." He may try to keep the partner from having a phone, or car, and try to keep her from working or going to school.

6. BLAMES OTHERS FOR PROBLEMS AND FEELINGS

If he is chronically unemployed, someone is always doing him wrong, or out to get him. He may make mistakes and then blame her for upsetting him and keeping him from concentrating on work. He may tell her she is at fault for anything that goes wrong. He may tell the partner, "You made me mad," or "You're hurting me by not doing what I want you to do," or "I can't help being angry," and "It's your fault that I hit you."

7. HYPERSENSITIVITY

An abuser is easily insulted. He claims his feelings are hurt when really, he's very mad. He takes the slightest setbacks as personal attacks. He may rant and rave about the injustice of things that have happened- things that are just part of life, like being asked to work overtime, getting a traffic ticket, being told a behavior is annoying, or being asked to help with chores.

8. CRUELTY TO ANIMALS OR CHILDREN

The abuser is a person who punishes animals brutally or is insensitive to their pain or suffering, he may expect children to be capable of doing things beyond their ability (e.g. spanking a two-year-old for wetting a diaper) or he may tease children until they cry (60% of abusers, who beat their domestic partners, also beat the children in the home). He may not want children to eat at the table or may expect them to stay in their rooms all evening while he is home.

9. "PLAYFUL" USE OF FORCE IN SEX

This kind of abuser may enjoy throwing the woman down and holding her down during sex. He may act out fantasies during sex where the woman is helpless. He lets her know the idea of rape is exciting. He may show little concern about whether or not she wants to have sex and uses sulking or anger to manipulate her into compliance. He may start having sex with the woman while she is asleep, or demand sex when she is ill or tired.

10. VERBAL ABUSE

In addition to saying things that are meant to be cruel and hurtful, the abuser may be degrading, vulgar, and run down the partner's accomplishments. He may curse her or call her names. He may tell the partner she is stupid and unable to function without him.

11. RIGID SEX ROLES

The abuser expects his partner to serve him. He may say the woman must stay at home, and she must obey him in all things, including engaging in criminal acts. The abuser sees women as inferior to men, responsible for menial tasks, stupid, and unable to be a whole person without a male partner.

12. DR. JEKYLL AND MR. HYDE

Many partners are confused by their abuser's sudden changes in mood- they may think the abuser has some special mental problem because one moment he is nice and the next moment he is exploding. Explosiveness and moodiness are typical of people who beat their partners, and these behaviors are related to other characteristics such as hypersensitivity.

13. PAST BATTERING

An abuser may have hit women in the past but say, "She

made me do it." The abuser's partner may hear stories of abusive behavior from relatives, ex-spouses, or girlfriends. A batterer will beat any woman he is with; situational circumstances do not make a person abusive.

14. BREAKING, THROWING, OR STRIKING OBJECTS

This behavior is used as punishment (breaking loved possessions) but is mostly used to terrorize the partner and cause her to submit to him. The abuser may beat tables with his fists, punch walls, or throw objects at the partner, all signs of extreme emotional immaturity. When the abuser thinks he has the right to punish or frighten his partner, the partner is in danger.

15. ANY FORCE DURING AN ARGUMENT

The abuser may hold the partner down, physically restraining her from leaving the room, or may push and shove her. He may hold the woman against the wall, saying, "You're going to listen to me!" He may take her car keys.

Warning Signs for Teens

From RAINN (Rape, Abuse, Incest National Network)
1-800-656-HOPE (4673) – https://www.rainn.org y rainn.org/es

If you're involved in the lives of adolescents, you can learn to recognize warning signs that a teen has been sexually assaulted or abused. Studies show that ages twelve to thirty-four are the highest risk years for crimes of sexual violence, and that females ages sixteen to nineteen are four times more likely than the general population to be victims of these crimes.[1] If you can learn how to spot sexual assault or abuse, you can do something to help.

Signs that a teen may have been sexually abused

Some of the warning signs that a teen has been sexually assaulted or abused can easily blend in with the everyday struggles teens face as they learn how to relate to their bodies, peers, and environments. If something doesn't seem right, trust your instincts. It's better to ask and be wrong than to let a teen struggle with the effects of sexual assault. Remind the teen that if they come to you, you will believe them—and that if something happened, it isn't their fault.

If you notice the following warning signs in a teen, it's worth reaching out to them.

- Unusual weight gain or weight loss
- Unhealthy eating patterns, like a loss of appetite or excessive eating
- Signs of physical abuse, such as bruises
- Sexually transmitted infections (STIs) or other genital infections
- Signs of depression, such as persistent sadness, lack of energy, changes in sleep or appetite, withdrawing from normal activities, or feeling "down"
- Anxiety or worry
- Falling grades
- Changes in self-care, such as paying less attention to hygiene, appearance, or fashion than they usually do
- Self-harming behavior

- Expressing thoughts about suicide or suicide behavior
- Drinking or drug use

Warning signs that a teen may be in an abusive relationship

It can be challenging for teens, who are new to dating, to recognize that sexual assault and abuse may be part of an abusive relationship. As someone outside of the relationship, you have the potential to notice warning signs that someone may be in abusive relationship or at risk for sexual assault.

Look for signs that a teen's boyfriend, girlfriend, or partner has done or said the following:

- Tries to get them to engage in sexual activity that they aren't ready for
- Sexually assaults them or coerces them into unwanted sexual activity
- Refuses to use contraception or protection against STIs during sexual activity
- Hits them or physically harms them in any way
- Doesn't want them spending time with friends or family
- Makes threats or controls their actions
- Uses drugs or alcohol to create situations where their judgement is impaired or compromises their ability to say "yes" or "no"

Using technology to hurt others

Teens may also experience sexual harassment or other

unwanted behaviors through technology and online interactions. Some people use technology—such as digital photos, videos, apps, and social media—to engage in harassing, unsolicited, or non-consensual sexual interactions. It can leave the person on the other end feeling manipulated, unsafe, and exposed, like when someone forwards a text, photo, or "sext" intended only for the original recipient. The laws pertaining to these situations vary from state to state and platform to platform, and they are evolving rapidly. Learn more about these how people use technology to harm others.

Taking action isn't easy, but it's important

Open communication can be a challenge with teens, but it's an important part of keeping them safe. As teens become more independent and spend more time with friends and other activities, it's important to keep the lines of communication open and let your teen know they can trust you. Learn more about talking to kids and teens about sexual assault.

Remember, you're not alone. If you suspect sexual abuse, you can talk to someone who is trained to help. Call the National Sexual Assault Hotline at 800.656.HOPE (4673) or chat online at online.rainn.org.

Department of Justice, Office of Justice Programs, Bureau of Justice Statistics, Sex Offenses and Offenders (1997).

❖❖❖

Talking to Your Kids About Sexual Assault

From RAINN (Rape, Abuse, Incest National Network)
1-800-656-HOPE (4673) – https://www.rainn.org y rainn.org/es

It can be stressful to plan a big safety talk about sexual assault with your kid. The good news is, you don't have to. Conversations about sexual assault can be a part of the safety conversations you're already having, like knowing when to speak up, how to take care of friends, and listening to your gut. The key is to start these conversations when your kids are young and have these conversations often.

Start conversations about safety when your kids are young

Teach young children the language they need to talk about their bodies and information about boundaries to help them understand what is allowed and what is inappropriate. These lessons help them know when something isn't right and give them the power to speak up.

- **Teach children the names of their body parts.** When children have the words to describe their body parts, they may find it easier to ask questions and express concerns about those body parts.
- **Some parts of the body are private.** Let children know that other people shouldn't touch or look at them. If a healthcare professional has to examine these parts of the body, be present.
- **It's okay to say "no."** It's important to let children know they are allowed to say "no" to touches that make them uncomfortable. This message isn't obvious to children, who are often taught to be obedient and follow the rules. Support your child if they say

no, even if it puts you in an uncomfortable position. For example, if your child doesn't want to hug someone at a family gathering, respect their decision to say "no" to this contact.

- **Talk about secrets.** Perpetrators will often use secret-keeping to manipulate children. Let children know they can always talk to you, especially if they've been told to keep a secret. If they see someone touching another child, they shouldn't keep this secret, either. Learn more about protecting a child from sexual assault.

- **Reassure them that they won't get in trouble.** Young children often fear getting in trouble or upsetting their parents by asking questions or talking about their experiences. Be a safe place for your child to share information about things that they have questions about or that make them uncomfortable. Remind them they won't be punished for sharing this information with you.

- **Show them what it looks like to do the right thing.** It could be as simple as helping an elderly person get off a bus or picking up change that someone has dropped on the ground. When you model helping behavior, it signals to your child that this is a normal, positive way to behave.

- **When they come to you, make time for them.** If your kid comes to you with something he or she feels is important, take the time to listen. Give them your undivided attention and let them know you take their concerns seriously. They may be more likely to come to you in the future if they know their voice will be heard.

Continue to engage teens in safety conversations

- It's important to create a dialogue about topics like

safety and sexual assault with your teen. Consider these conversation starters to engage them in conversation.

- **Use the media to make it relevant.** Ask your teen's opinion on something happening on social media, in the news, in a new movie, or on a popular TV show. You could even watch an episode with them and ask follow up questions. Asking their opinion shows them that you value their point of view and opens up the door for more conversation.
- **Use your own experience to tell a safety story.** Sharing your own experiences can make these conversations relevant and feel more real to teens. If you don't have an experience you feel comfortable sharing, you can tell a story about someone you know.
- **Talk about caring for their friends- not just about their own behavior.** Talking about how to be a good friend can be a powerful way of expressing to your teen that you trust them to do the right thing without sounding like you're targeting their personal behavior. It also gives you the chance to communicate safety practices they may not otherwise be receptive to.
- **Talk about sexual assault directly.** For some teens, safety issues like sexual assault aren't on the radar. On the other hand, they may have misconceptions about sexual assault they've picked up from peers or the media. Bring up statistics that relate to them, such as the fact that ninety-three percent of victims who are minors know the perpetrator. Explain that no one "looks like a rapist," and that seven out of ten instances of sexual assault are committed by someone known to the victim.

To speak with someone who is trained to help, call the National Sexual Assault Hotline at 800.656.HOPE (4673) or chat online at online.rainn.org. For additional information on talking with your child about safety from sexual abuse, visit Darkness to Light.

Check Out Other Books and Pages by the Author, Martha Duke Anderson!

Facebook Author Page: *Martha Duke Anderson Books*
"Like" the page to receive notifications of upcoming releases.

Golden Threads, the novel
One Woman's Journey That Will Change Her Life Forever

After her mother's death, Mona, heartbroken and selfabsorbed, moves in with Gran when she can't make it on her own. It's a big change from her Army-kid upbringing. Intriguing and superstitious Gran tells fascinating old family stories, but not the one Mona most needs to hear.

Mona meets John and Lennie through her work. Both vie for her love, but each has his own challenge that prevents Mona from freely giving her heart. Will mild-mannered Gran ever be able to tell Mona the unspoken truth that could change everything with her two handsome suitors?

Through laughter and tears, Mona discovers a growing love and admiration for older folks, and for both men, but which man will win her love?

Fans of *Fried Green Tomatoes,* and *The Help* will enjoy this family saga love story that connects the generations with love. Watch for the sequel, Golden Threads Shining Bright.

Praise for Golden Threads

"Martha has woven together a wonderful story filled with endearing characters, many of whom are seniors who both need support, but also give support to Mona, and in so doing

change her life for the better. This story provides homegrown inspiration for young and old alike, insight on navigating relationships across generations, help for people in need, and a sprinkling of wonderful recipes. It will warm your heart!"
Sandy Markwood, Chief Executive Officer, National Association of Area Agencies on Aging

"Seniors and young people have warped perceptions of each other. Youth think old people are slow and scary; seniors see youth as noisy and troublesome. *Golden Threads* demonstrates what happens when you put the two groups together in meaningful and respectful ways."
Lawayne Childrey, Author of Peeling Back the Layers: A Story of Trauma, Grace and Triumph; and a recipient of the national Edward R. Murrow Award for Journalistic Excellence.

"The stories woven within *Golden Threads* take the reader by the hand to a journey into the South's past. A journey filled with lore, laughter, and sometimes tears. Through it all, we grow and learn, along with the main character, Mona, to honor the lives of those who truly lived. Ms. Anderson's voice is uniquely southern, and endearing. This is a journey you'll want to take."
Linda Edmondson Ward, Non-Profit Program Director

Golden Threads Shining Bright

Golden Threads Shining Bright, the sequel to *Golden Threads,* is coming soon! Sign up to get a notification of when the sequel becomes available. To find out what happens next with Mona, John, Gran, Lacey, and Wiley, and to discover more of their recipes, visit www.marthadukeanderson.com and sign up.

Also Coming Soon!

Golden Threads Shine Forever, Book 3 in the *Golden Threads Trilogy; and Caregiver Tips and Tales*, a book for Caregivers

Visit www.marthadukeanderson.com and sign up for notifications.

Celebrate Golden Images

You are invited to check out **Celebrate Golden Images**, Martha's Facebook tribute page respecting, honoring, and valuing the lives of older adults, age sixty or more, through photos. You might like to post a friend or relative or just enjoy the photos! Any age may join, but the photos posted are of our Golden-agers. Thanks for checking it out.

On Facebook, search for **Celebrate Golden Images** or use this link: www.facebook.com/groups/1679082692403200/

Website: www.marthadukeanderson.com

Email: mdanderson.5000@gmail.com

Facebook: https://www.facebook.com/marthadukeanderson/
Author Page
Amazon: www.amazon.com/author/martha.duke.anderson
Author Page
Celebrate: www.facebook.com/groups/1679082692403200/

Golden Images
Twitter: https://mobile.twitter.com/MarthaDA5000
Instagram: www.instagram.com/martha.5000

About the Author ~ Martha Duke Anderson

Riding on a mule-drawn wagon, on a dirt road in Southeast Alabama with her grandpa, thrilled five-year-old Martha Anderson. The daily lives of her grandparents, and the memories told by them, deeply anchored Martha in love and respect for them and other older people.

Martha Anderson, the author, says, "I have a deep affinity for older people, and the disadvantaged. I believe in honoring, respecting, and valuing the lives of others."

Martha earned degrees in psychology and criminal justice. She is a licensed social worker, a former certified long-term care ombudsman, and a certified information and resource specialist with a certificate in aging and disability.

Prior to writing books, Martha worked for thirty years at an Area Agency on Aging (AAA). She became an expert in aging and disability programs, case management, and benefits and entitlements. She retired as the Director of Home and Community Services at the Southern Alabama Regional Council on Aging (SARCOA). Martha, through her work, garnered achievement awards for SARCOA, from the National Association of Area Agencies on Aging (N4A).

Manufactured by Amazon.ca
Bolton, ON

42414046R00155